D0920625

****

LONDON

or, The Anatomy of Melancholy

a novel

MATTHEW SELWYN

First edition

This book is a work of fiction. Names, characters, businesses, organisatons, places, events, and incidents are the product either of the author's imagination or are used fictitiously. Any resemblence to actual persons, living or dead, events, or locales is entirely coincidental.

Copyright © Matthew Selwyn

The right of Matthew Selwyn to be identified as author of this work has been asserted by him in accordance with the Copyright, Designs and Patents Act 1998.

All rights reserved. Published in the United Kingdom by Electric Reads, London.

www.electricreads.com

ISBN (print): 978-0-9931305-0-2
ISBN (MOBI eBook): 978-0-9931305-1-9
ISBN (ePub eBook): 978-0-9931305-2-6

All rights reserved. Apart from any use under UK copyright law no part of this publication may be reproduced, stored in a retrieval system, or transmitted, in any form or by any means, without prior written permission of the publisher, nor be otherwise circulated in any form of binding or cover other than that in which it is published and without a similar condition being imposed on the subsequent publisher.

10 9 8 7 6 5 4 3 2 1

****

THE CHEMIST WAS CLOSED, so I went to the movies instead; fat lot of good that did me. They don't half put some morbid shit on nowadays; even the robots blowing each other apart stop every five minutes to stroke their psyches and fiddle with their ids. Christ, what happened to mindless violence, or happy endings? When did we give up the pretence?

This wind tonight; cutting across my face, bringing reluctant tears to my eyes. Five minutes from home, but it feels like an age until I'll be back in the warm. The street lamps light the way; two more streets and I'm there. Normally I'd savour the night, the electricity of the dark as everything gains that sheen, reaches its potential.

It's not a night to claim the streets though – the weather's too rough for most – so what the fuck are all these pikeys doing hanging about? Course, you can't call them pikeys anymore, not unless you know who you're talking to. But you're fine, you'll do. They can eye me all they like; I'm a stringy bastard, but I'll fucking have them if they try anything with me. Yeah, even the tall one, with the leer. I'm not afraid of a little violence. And when it comes down to it, that's what really matters.

Most people, see, they think in violence, but they don't know the half; you gotta go in hard with people like that. When you see it in their eyes – that unknown, that fear – you gotta split a lip or better still bust an eyebrow, fast. Soon as they feel warm blood dripping down their face they get that lurch in their stomach, that sinking dread of what might come. They don't want any more then. You gotta be careful though - you don't want to fight either, if you can help it.

These boys here; most of them have probably never known what it feels like to have teeth ripped from your jaw as a fist slams into your cheek, but some might. And even if they don't, groups is different. When it's you against a group, they get all this boldness, see, think they're hard because their mates are around. Best to avoid groups; you don't want any part of that. But if it comes to it – and don't pull this until you know it's definitely on – you gotta be wild, real wild, and scream. Scares the shit out of people that; they don't expect it, see. Scream like you're about to rip their fucking heart out, like you're ready to chew the skin from their faces. Oh, you won't have any problems then, my friend; then you can split a few lips and they'll soon call it a night. Doesn't matter what the odds are; ten against one feral bastard and there'll still be casualties on both sides and everyone knows it. Most people don't want to gamble.

These twats here, they aren't in it for the violence; they're in it for the money. It didn't use to be this way, so the old timers say at least. Used to be a time when lads would go out looking for a fight – just a fight – wanting to feel the burn of violence. But violence is a business now. People don't do it to feel alive; they do it to stay alive. Crime's a transaction; no one wants violence, so you hand over your money and they withhold their service. Sometimes someone doesn't know the rules of the game, or they forget the etiquette – then it kicks off. Normally a little shoving at first, maybe a slap – that puts most people in line. What happens then, well, that kind of depends on the group.

Hang about and we might get to find out here. This little gang, these corporate criminals, they're preparing for their next customer. *Customers*, actually: a couple, winding their way towards them. The guy is pretty big from a distance. Hard to tell if it's fat or muscle, but his little lady is hiding away under his arm like a right little Mary. Oh she thinks she's safe alright, in the armpit of this great bear. She doesn't know the half. These are the new days, love, nobody gets a pass anymore. You have to stump up like the rest of us; your man can't help you out here. No one can.

Christ, they're moving slowly though. Maybe they see the danger, maybe their minds are willing them to turn back but their feet are still moving, pushing past the impulse. They need to get a shake on. I don't want to miss this, but I'm not slowing up any more. This is not a night to idle along with your love, love; get your fella's great, lumbering body moving.

Even the boys are getting impatient; some are edging

their way up the street, pulled unknowingly towards their target. Clearly this couple don't know the rules of the game; they should have turned back long ago and chosen another path, or else showed a little more conviction in their decision. This creeping pace, this edging towards the act; it's nothing but a tease. The inevitable is already in motion, the boys are in too deep now; their angst is up, they're committed. The longer this drags out, the more chance there is for violence. Nobody wants that. Not out here, in reality, and reality doesn't come any realer than this.

* * * *

Is it all about tits? A lot of guys will tell you that, but they're crass; they don't really get it. If you listened to them you'd think women should be judged just on their cup size. There's so much more to it, so much more to tits even: the shape, the feel, the aesthetics, and that's just for starters. That's just the obvious. But then, that's what men are – obvious – isn't it? Millions upon millions of websites out there, and when men want to find something to jack off to, what do they search for? Tits. If they're being creative: Big Tits. I mean fuck. Centuries of social evolution and what they want is tits, big tits.

But at least that's straight-forward, there's nothing mysterious about what gets a guy sprung; girls know where they stand in the grand scheme. It's not so easy for us guys; you can't whip your cock out and size yourself up. It doesn't mean a thing. You can be a limp dick loser in the sack and girls won't care; it doesn't compute. Or you can be a huge swinging dick like me, perfect record, and it doesn't get you there any faster, doesn't give you any clue where you rank. Women, they just don't get it, they don't see how simple life is, how simple it should be.

Lexi's not so bad. Ok, she goes in for all that emotional nonsense, but talk about a rack – Christ, she's got a pair. They're not the biggest tits you've ever seen – a handful for sure – but talk about perfectly formed. Smooth as a babe's arse and with just a little droop – not too much, still pert, but just enough that there's a good amount of bounce when you fuck her. See, this is where a true connoisseur, like myself, and your regular dick-in-hand loser differ; it's the appreciation of the subtleties of the female form.

But don't think I'm all about Lexi's tits and nothing else – she's got a whole lot more going on. She's this demure little Scottish gint, and yeah, I know what you're thinking: Scottish equals dour cunt – well you can fuck right off with that. She's the real deal: harsh jaw; freckles; wide, cool blue eyes; slim body and flowing brown curls. Oh yes, my friend, an absolute A+ dame with world-class norks thrown in – my wee Scotch stunner. And isn't that the kick-in-the-balls, funny as fuck thing? All your life you look to America for those home-grown, corn-fed tits that the Yank bitches all sprout when they're about fourteen – those bulging DDs that you wank about as a kid as you look longingly across the Atlantic, simultaneously repulsed and electrified – and then the greatest tits you've ever seen walk straight out of Giffnock (Glasgow, but you knew that, right?) and bounce their sweet way down to you via the Caledonian-sleeper train. I know they say America is finished, but Christ, when the Jock lassies are packing the premium chest meat, you know they aren't kidding.

Oh, and they might tell you that all the true beauties come from the East – the former Baltic states, where old Stalin must have fucked around with eugenics or something, because the production line of stacked broads is out of this world, but I'd put Lexi up against any of those Pole sluts who'll drop their knickers for a fistful of Yank dollars. Lexi's different – she's hot as fuck, but she's sweet too. She'll suck your balls dry and make you dinner afterwards – that's Lex. Cool as.

* * * *

My soles kiss the pavement – a gentle smack as plastic meets concrete and I propel myself forward, avoiding jutting paving slabs, broken glass: the debris of life as we know it.

My heart thumps as hot energy floods through my limbs. I breathe heavy, rattling breaths, and drive forwards. Around me the world blurs into a wash of colours, and I fix my gaze – try not to look to either side, but glare straight forward, where things are more distinct, less of a haze. I focus my attention and try desperately not to think of what's behind, what's around me. Forwards, always forwards.

* * * *

Soft, warm smoke fills my lungs, drifting from between Lexi's perfect lips and billowing out between us into the night air. I close the gap, drink in the soothing vapour. My hands on her waist, Lex continues to take long drags on her cigarette, bringing it up between us and inhaling the poison while looking me square in the eye.

I feel her small hand creeping up my inner thigh – toying with my jeans as she glides towards the semi I'm already sporting. The low, growling beat of the music seeps out from the club. Girls giggle as they stumble from the front door, the bouncers enjoying a good eyeful as they go. I look over, but no one's interested in us; we're just one of many couples out here, each stuck somewhere between the dance floor and bed.

I look back. Lexi flicks her stub into the gutter and, her hand sliding over my cock, grabs me by the hand and pulls me back into the blur of the nightclub.

A wall of noise hits as soon as we step through the door: the furious lights and angry beats thumping throughout. Make no mistake; clubs are places of aggression, of violent expression. Lexi leads the way back to the dance floor. Cutting a path through the crowd, guys and girls alike pause in their furious movement to cop an eyeful of Lex's bulging cleavage: the world stops for big tits. We hit a spot clear enough to make our own. Bodies around us in seizures of ecstatic freedom, we stake our claim; take ownership of the floor. Few of our fellow exhibitionists stop to acknowledge the new centre of the room – not openly – but they feel the fresh pull, the new gravity.

Thrusting hands through her mussed hair, Lexi narrows her eyes – enough to create the impression of blindness, not enough to stop her knowing what's going on around her – and rocks her hips slowly to the music. As I move in to join her, I feel the soft pressure of a hand at my side. I turn.

A blonde with high cheek bones and Nordic looks smiles up at me. Her face is familiar, but I can't place her. Likely, we've done the dirty, but who can keep track? I grin as she turns and presses her firm rump into me, gyrating as the music infects her body.

I look over to Lexi and see her moving towards us – calm, but prepared for the scrap. She knows the score – we both do – it's a meat market out here, and you've gotta expect competition for premium sirloin.

Running her hand faintly across my face and down my shoulder, Lexi glides straight past me and pulls the pocket Barbie away. Wrapping her slim arms around the blonde, Lexi presses herself close – her breasts squashing against the bony shoulder blades of her partner. The two writhe together, Lexi driving blondie's hips and running one of her hands through the mass of bleached hair in front of her. Blondie's eyes close as she rocks her head back into her partner, but Lexi looks only at me.

I breathe heavy, the air thick with sweat and sex. Lexi pulls away from Barbie and, giving her a small pat on the bum, pushes her back into the heaving crowd. I look on as the whip of blonde hair disappears into the mass that surrounds us, and then there is only Lex.

Her rich breath, still thick with tobacco, engulfs me as she presses me close. Grabbing her wrist, I pull her to the back of the club, to our only chance of privacy.

Slamming the door to the disabled toilet behind us, I throw my tiny nymph against the wall, and press up against her – the weight of my body reminding her of the eternal truth of our relationship, of every relationship. Lifting her legs so they're wrapped around me, I press against her, trapping her in the embrace. Pushing my hot lips away, she pauses – places her forefinger against my mouth and reaches into her the left cup of her over-full bra.

She pulls out a tiny packet of blow; the soft whiteness of the powder highlighting the grime of the surfaces around us. I step back and release Lex, let her cut the stuff.

Rolling a loose bill, she stoops and inhales a line. Then another.

Don't worry, I get my share.

The fresh, raw feeling overwhelms. The blood flows, and we fuck, right there amongst the grime.

* * * *

There's a problem here. You're not daft; you see it, you understand my plight. Shit, we all feel it – it's in every atom of the world around us, each breath we take more suffocating than the last. The churning sickness that is

19

life – the wonderful tangle, the mess of existence. Step right up for the ride of your life, join the bandwagon, come on board. You, me, we're all in – there is no opt out. That's our problem; we're stuck firmly in time, rooted in reality.

* * * *

I love the mornings. That clear, fresh air that you don't get after midday, let alone in the smoky evenings when the game commences and the lambs scatter across the town centres, eager for the wolves to try their luck but scared that the tease might work. You've gotta get out in this true air, drink it in, embrace the clear-headed crispness of the world before it's polluted by the people who soil it daily. Stomping up the high road with cars beeping and hollering, you wouldn't think you'd find any peace, but you're not looking hard enough; perhaps you're just not in tune with the city. This is life, my friend; that countryside bullshit that you see in the films, it doesn't exist anymore. This is it. The jungle, the noise, the heaving, whirling spread. Drink it in: the new air that accompanies the new day. We can all sense it: the freshness, the possibilities the newly birthed day brings.

The conveyor belt of traffic files neatly past: ma's roll steadily down the hill in gleaming tanks, ferrying their tykes to some cunty private school or other. Slick bastards dart, agitated, between the rows of traffic; erections pressing against their designer suits as they finger the gear sticks of their German sports cars, primed to hit the accelerator and slide into a gap that barely exists.

Sometimes you'll get an alien in the mix. Not your regular nine-to-fiver. Oh, it all kicks off then. They need to wise up; or stay out of the tangle. This is not the time to creep around or look for sympathy. You can't expect that from the people here, boxed off from the world in their cold wombs, which carry them around from place to place. They aren't interested; they don't carry passengers. If you're not in on the game, you need to move along. The blare of a horn lets you know that someone's out of their depth. Or that one of the cock slingers has shot their load prematurely; misread the signs, jumped when there was nothing to jump for.

In the distance, a siren sounds and lights flash. In the game, no one moves. We don't give way to ambulances anymore. We're all sick, all suffering an emergency. Flashing lights don't give you priority these days. Urgency doesn't mean much.

The drivers involved in this game are focused, they don't see much outside of their tunnel vision. Certainly not me, a pedestrian: I'm not a participant, just one of the bystanders. Occasionally a ma will drag her wretches between the cars as they edge forward in a perfect assembly line, one steel cage following another. She can risk entering the game you see, with little Tommy hanging on to her leggings and Shenice struggling to escape the confines of her own plastic cage. If Ma misjudges it, if none of the drivers yield and let her pass as she pushes her buggy impetuously forward across stream, her problems are halved at worst. If that happens, the real losers are those on the conveyor belt. The hold up while the game is reset.

So you see, I'm good here, I'm great. I can glide along this pavement and no one gives a damn; there's no crossover. I could be bollock-naked and no one would bother a moment. As it is, I'm happy stalking down the hill in these old khakis, jacket pulled tight around me. There's spit in the air and it's not a day to tread the streets. Nothing good happens in this weather; the half-arsed, weak as piss in-between of a grey English winter's morning. You can't be present in this shit; you've got to escape to the world. Take a trip.

* * * *

I hate the underground. Whoever designed the carriages must have been a sick bastard – rows of awkward people, each sat staring at complete strangers across the aisle, trying to avoid eye contact while appraising everything about the cunts opposite: small, boring people. And that's on a good day. Try sitting face to crotch with some yuppie throwback who's taking the train because his wank-mobile is in the garage. Imagine being face with that as the overground descends underground, the flaking concrete of battered and outdated buildings replaced by the claustrophobic, crumbling brickwork of the tunnels that flash by. Stuck in the false intimacy of the setting with these pricks.

But it's the train today. Seven stops to negotiate. Twenty minutes being shuttled around the bowels of London with the excrement it's accumulated from its foreign adventures. If I time my journey right I'll be able to hop the gate at the station as the luminous wanker in the office waddles off to be replaced by some other poe-faced jobsworth. Once you're on the train, you're alright. At the other end – once you're in the City – you can flash any ticket you like at the gate. Force of numbers, see, the guards checking tickets don't take in the individuals; you just become part of the crowd, gliding around in an atomic mass.

But you can only complain about the transport in London so much. Any system that lets you get from a to b without paying a penny can't be bad. Freedom of movement, and that. Granted, you get the odd anal attendant who demands a ticket before offering you a penalty instead. Sure, that's a pain. Especially the late night ones, when you've got a warm pussy waiting on you, and some Malcolm demands that you invent an identity to put on his form. It's a hassle.

* * * *

A little sight-seeing on the way to the gallery: two French birds with sweet derrieres and some Latin chick with huge maracas. It's always the tourists at this time in the morning. Wait until after lunch, when all the Slovaks get out from their cleaning jobs – that's when you see the real quality. The broads who've been here for years but still earn £3.20 an hour scrubbing bogs, hoping that some boy from the old country will pick them up and keep them in Prada until they can slip a pregnancy on them. They'd be lucky. Even if they've got half a body (and most of them do under those overalls) the best they can hope for is a semi-connected guy who thinks he's hot shit because he drives a clapped-out Mercedes E class and wears a chain thicker than his cock. If a dame hasn't got one of those tight, Baltic bodies, they're as good as screwed. They might end up with some 90-hour a week plumber or a comrade with middle-aged spread and a grimy taxi business. But, look, don't be disheartened; there's always the chance these broads will come across some home-grown, balding dickweed who lives in his mother's old council flat, and who will be all too willing to exchange vows for a bi-annual blowjob. That's the ideal — the comfortable life: the supportive and pussy-whipped loser. Miss Visa-whore gets her nails done regularly, doesn't work a dime apart from when she's sucking dick or out hustling with her girls on a Friday night while her husband stays home beating it off to a fuzzy porno on his old VCR.

But you probably know the shakes, right? I don't need to tell you how this stuff works; you're alive, you've seen it all a million times.

* * * *

Was Flaubert always a wanker, or just when it came to Emma Bovary? You've gotta wonder about these arty types who sit about cupping their balls and congratulating themselves on their own brilliance as they spunk out a load of art. Don't get me wrong, some of it is proper genius. But let's be honest, most of it's a con, isn't it? These loners who hide away from the world, telling us – the people of the world – that they're interpreting it all for us. Showing us truths that we can't see for ourselves. And then – and this is where the whole racket really sings – you get a whole bunch of speccy cunts who wish they could get away with that shit, but can't, so instead heap praise on the people who're already on the inside in the hope that they can get in on the act: it's a never-ending cycle of mutual masturbation, with the current lot propping up the con of those who went before them, and paving the way for the next generation. We should fucking have 'em. Get rid of the lot.

I might be an ignorant twat, but this bird here ain't anything to look at. Plump, barely any tits. Whoever painted her obviously hadn't put it about much because let me tell you, there are some corkers out there, and this dame is ten a penny. If this wanker had ever bothered to go out and dip his cock like the rest of us, he'd have spewed out some proper works of art. And don't get me wrong, he can obviously paint. There's talent there, but fuck; if he'd just lived a little! If I could paint like that, I'd turn some heads, put Lexi up there on a canvas. Drawing isn't my thing; it's for old women and cunty Europeans, but give me a decent camera and I'll show you what you can do with a woman's body. None of these fat birds lounging around on leaves and that.

The thing that gets me is all these trendy pansies who bring their squeezes round and whisper in their ears as they look over the elaborate cons that cover the walls. It's a means to an end, I'll give you that. I've even considered it myself, but honestly, there are quicker ways into a pair of knickers. And these arty girls, they don't want a real man, they want a soppy, dickless twat, with long hair and a sweet voice. If they had a balls-deep fucker like me they'd shit their pants.

Don't think it's just the young who get carried away with all this either. Wait 'til you see the grey brigade on the march. Breathing peppermint breath over all the staff as they stop to ask for directions, they're as bad as the greasy twats. They're not lost; they're just on a jolly. Everyone knows it; we're all colluding. Even me, sitting here in front of these 'masterpieces', watching out for skirt and trying to understand the rules of this game. I'm almost there – I've almost got a handle on how these galleries work – but every now and then something throws a spanner in the works. Last year, when I was just getting a grip on all this 'art', I sat just over the hall, watching the balls-out conspirators schlep around, not ashamed but brazen. There were more than normal, and I followed the masses, not wanting to miss an opportunity to understand the collective delusion these lemmings shared.

Everyone was heading to the final room in the gallery, and when I got there I found these sprawling canvases; just three or four set apart on the far wall. The rich colours, the disorienting images: for a while I stopped colluding and started believing. I sat for ages in that room, looking around the people and trying to understand this form of expression. It really got into your senses, let you breathe it in; it had something true in a way that the other imposters just didn't.

Since then I've wondered if there was something to this stuff, something more than the obvious. Perhaps the people who use it like words are the ones who hold the rest back. If they all knew what me and Salvador did they'd drop the lumpy dames and put their cocks to some better use.

But look, if you think art is all a con, try having a nosey around one of these gallery's cafes. There's a laugh. £4.50 for a slice of stale chocolate cake – Jesus. £3.00 for a cup of coffee – pissed out fresh that morning. The people who run these places – shit, they're onto something. They collect all these soppy fags who want to pretend to be a bit 'cultural' together and shake them down, rinse them out. If the mob had any sense they'd get into this boutique robbery. People don't want the grime of life anymore; will pay anything to avoid it. These places, they're just a safe haven for the weak. It's a perfect racket.

* * * *

How do one-woman men survive? How do they allow themselves to buy into the female bullshit that is monogamy? It's a smart idea, I'll grant you. Women, as much as they like to bleat on about being oppressed and all that, well, they have more say about how this world is run than they let on. Monogamy – that's no man's idea, no chance. It goes against our nature – humans that is, not just men. Everyone knows it deep down: all the frilly pretence and picture-perfect love stories, they're all part of the illusion.

No, we're all in it for ourselves, we like the variety that polygamy brings, but we're terrified of a world where it rules, where no one can claim ownership over another person. Bit fucking sad, no? Well, some of us don't buy into all that, some of us see beyond and realise that change is coming, like it or not. You can't stop progress, can't stop us fighting towards our true nature.

So what's your running total, my friend – how many notches on your bed post? No need to be shy, I'm not expecting triple figures or anything. See, you're fine, you're no fool, but most people, well, they just don't have what it takes, do they? It's the physical, the mental, the emotional – they've all got to line up if you want to live the New Life. It's hardly surprising that there's only a select few adapted for that shit.

Me, I've had more girls than you can count. I'm out there in front of the ordinary, leading the curve. Tracy, Flora, Jessica – you name it, I've had a go. And these are premium booty – no cheap rejects here, pal. You've got to be discerning when there's the whole world to choose from; it's not enough to just go with them that make it easy, ones that are clacking for it. No, you've gotta pace yourself, enjoy the selection. Wasting time on the mediocre, it's energy badly spent.

Fair play, when you start out there's always going to be a learning curve. I remember the first time I got down to the necessary with a girl – Jenna – she was a right stunner: blonde, big tits. Well, so I thought at the time, looking back now I realise that she was just a fantasy: she had all the right components, but they didn't add up to what a connoisseur appreciates as real quality. That's the difference, isn't it? Most people, see, they start out following the boring fantasy – seeking out the prescribed view of desirability in all aspects of life – it's the few that take this on and develop their own wants into something a little more sophisticated; they're the smart ones, my friend. Jenna's firm round breasts didn't snag me for that long – I quickly saw the need for variety.

Then there was Tera; she was a fine piece. She still had the glam appeal that Jenna was rocking, but she was a little more out there; thick Latin limbs and a dangerous look. She took me outside the mainstream, kept me interested a little longer than Jenna – there was never any question of it being a full-time thing, but it was fresh. Course, you realise soon enough that sorts like that, well, they're all the same really: Jenna, Tera – there were more too – they're all part of the mainstream if you're honest.

When you realise that, there's only one reaction – to thrust yourself away from the ordinary and seek out something on the margins. Some guys go for the anorexics who feel like they'll break if you handle them too rough, or the plumpers who are sturdy, who can take anything you've got to offer and remain unmoved. Other guys, they look for piercings, tattoos, some even go for disfigurements – anything to break the monotony of beauty. Sure, I've been there. It still appeals sometimes, but it's refined in me now – it's the subtle difference, not the dramatic.

Take Devon for example; she's all flailing limbs and awkwardness. You'd think it wouldn't be attractive but there's this unusual, pantomimic effect when you fuck someone like that – like it's a new form of art. Or, Alex with her giant snoz – it's the minor disfigurements that do it for the cultured. A great snout like that, bold and obtrusive, it draws the attention, makes you look at its owner with clear eyes. Most people, see, they don't get it – just want the picture-perfect. Course, that's the end-game, the highest goal, but you gotta go through the variety to appreciate the truly perfect.

Lexi, she's the new breed – a hybrid – neither mainstream nor outside of it. She's broken perfection, a fraying of the model, a dizzying mix of the desirable and the repugnant. Shit, you don't have to follow me on this one – how could you? But take my word for it – there's a whole ocean of fish out there and you need to get amongst it, my friend. Dive in and harpoon yourself as many swimmers as you can – your time won't last forever, and you've barely got started.

* * * *

Press the sound deep – it's the only way to hear. These tiny earbuds don't stand a chance against the roar of the city – nothing does – but stuff them in deep, volume up, and you might escape. It's not that you can drown out the world, it's more that you can tell it to fuck off. When one of the scroungers looks your way they know the score: the noise surrounds you, protects you – you're not there to engage, you don't want them to penetrate the barrier.

Everyone knows this – it's human nature. You don't go pulling someone out of their peace unless you've got a good reason. Behind the wall of screaming vocals you're safe. Am I listening to the beats? No. Is it to intimidate? Fuck yes. It's to say, 'Hey, I'm not like you, so don't think you have anything to say that I want to hear. I'm me and you're you, so let's keep it like that.'

Sometimes someone thinks they have the right to invade, to stake a claim on your time and your interest. They rarely do. If anyone tries to penetrate it's best to keep on going, to look past and shrug it off. If they're persistent, you might have to give them a look, or, if they're determined to break etiquette and force you to engage, you may have to explain how this shit works. A few choice words should do it – most people don't want engagement at any cost; they've all got their price, you've got to make sure it's not worth their while to try it.

So barriers up; I'm pretty safe from the ear-chewers and those that come at you, hands out, asking for a little kindness. Good luck, pal, there's not enough to go around and you're out. You're through. No, earphones are the first line of defence. I'll tell you what I don't get though, is those little fuckers – the ones whose balls haven't even dropped – who jolly round in groups, blasting that tinny music from their phones. They're claiming the space, planting a flag and saying this place, it's ours. Shit, they're welcome to it, the greasy pricks; no one's complaining. They can have the top deck of any bus they fancy, the corner of any station or cheap cafe. They can plant their flag, stake their claim, it's all theirs, because, after all, where's it getting them? They're open, exposed. The world focuses its gaze, looks on disgusted – they're a scapegoat to sneer at.

No, no, no, these little oinks haven't learnt, haven't realised the beauty of anonymity, of stealth. You don't want to march through life, drawing attention, it's no good – it forces the world to react, to embrace or repel. No, you want to slide by, to stay under the radar, unbothered, and never engaged.

I pause at the book stall under the bridge, take a moment to look over the tables covered in scruffy volumes. Whenever I get too close to another browser, I can feel the tension, the beats from my headphones drifting out and polluting their peace. They need to take a closer look around; I'm not polluting anything. What is there left to pollute? But there's no comeback, no recourse. They know this: they can tut and mutter into their hobo-boho-chic beards and grumble about it later with their Bordeaux-sipping friends, but that's it, that's all there is for them.

I love this place – it's a magnet for tweed wankers and middle-aged women looking for something to fill their lonely nights. It's a laugh. Oh yes, my friend, I'm a regular cultural anthropologist, if you please. They could slap a doctorate on me with the things I know about this world. All these men who think they're different, comfortable, individual. These women, who long to be part of something bigger, to homogenise. Jesus, don't they see it? Don't they open their eyes and wonder just exactly what the fuck they're doing with their lives?

* * * *

Eyes heavy in their sockets; a dulled complaint against the world, a plea for peace and darkness. It's barely eleven and I'm flagging – all-nighters aren't all they're cracked up to be. Alright, I'm on a promise – something to keep me on it – but this is still a drag. With nothing from the chemistry set to lighten the mood and brighten the eyes, I wait.

She should have been here half an hour ago. Lazy bitch. Probably thinks she's playing me, building up the tension. They all think they know this shit, how to drive guys wild – Cosmo decrees and they follow suit. Well, let me tell you something, she'd be driving me a whole lot wilder if she was here, grinding on my crotch to the heavy beats that the DJ sends flooding out, surrounding me.

Still, having the information from those Cosmo articles in the bank gives them some confidence, I guess. Lets them know what the game is all about – what the players are into – before they step into the arena. It's some warped shit, but there's something to it: a little teasing goes a long way. Chloe might be getting this one wrong, but she probably doesn't realise she's dealing with a guy who's seen it all before, who doesn't blink. If she had some sappy dickweed waiting on her, nursing a semi until she bothered to show up, she might be onto a winner. But that's not me. I'm not here to play their games, I'm here to live. Surrounded by noise, watching bodies writhing, I'm set. She can take her time. Someday they'll all realise that *Sex and the City* isn't how things go, that all this nonsense only delays the inevitable, the pleasure that makes the game worthwhile. Jesus. You'd think Cosmo would throw in a little reality every now and then.

And before you get carried away, let's get this straight: Chloe is a sweet girl and we have a good time, but she's not my type. Don't get me wrong, I like a bird with brains, but Chloe's a whole other thing – computer geek and then some – I'm not into that shit. Spending your life hunched over a keyboard, forgetting what the world is like out there: lack of sun, lack of life, your skin sallowing to the point of transparency. You can keep that shit. You need a bit of perspective. Sure, your laptop's a window to the world, but you wanna try your own front door – there's a whole lot more world out there – you'll love it! You've gotta keep things in balance, see. That's what I'm all about when it comes to the net: a little research on the people worth researching here, chat to some Yank teens there; but when all's said and done, you've gotta try life out for yourself. Open the door and give the world a shake, see what falls out.

See, me and Chloe, we're just mates, but I'm introducing her to a whole new world: the real world, the true world. Ok, she wants something more from me, you can just tell. She doesn't understand the life I lead, can't accept the fact that some of us don't want to be tied to one person for the rest of our days. Jesus, what a thought. Monogamy was a lot easier when you could count the alternatives on one hand. There's just no need for it anymore. Pop a condom on and knock yourself out, my friend. Where's the harm? We're all up for it, we all want a piece. Why restrict yourself, why limit the options? Chloe doesn't get it. If she did, the whole thing might be different. See, Lexi, she understands the game. Realises that the rules don't apply anymore – it's a free market and we're all buying.

Fuck it's hot in here; my t-shirt sticks to the sweat that engulfs my already aching body. Thirty-five minutes late now – jammy kraut. What happened to German efficiency? Thought you could set your watch by it. Still, Chloe's not what you'd call a 'proper German'. She doesn't buy into the culture. Alright, I can live without that aggressive shit. And I like a bit of warmth. But when it comes down to the necessary, the Krauts have got it right – they know how to treat a woman. We might turn to vanilla Yank flicks when we want to knock a quick one out – it's convenient – but we all know that the Germans do it better. Go and find your Dad's old VHS pornos, pal, you'll soon discover what fucking should be about.

Chloe's a funny little thing. Skinny as fuck, pale, with barely mosquito bite tits hidden away under her range of rock t-shirts, and black hair kept short but always a choppy mess. The conformity of the counter-culture. Like I said; not my type. But she's keen, that's always a bonus. And she feels the darkness. That's a pretty good combination for a hardcore shagging. But we don't. We just chat. That's our thing.

She's got some views, Chloe. A lot of it is pretty standard stuff, or bleating liberal bullshit. It's not a surprise – the plagiarised views, the too-familiar lines – it's a comfortable imprecision. See, people celebrate difference, originality. Well, in theory. In reality, what they want is conformity. They like the idea of someone swimming upstream, but not the reality. The moderns, the people like me, they'll never be accepted. The world isn't interested, it doesn't want to deal with different, it wants manufactured dissent, voices that reach only so far, have only so much to say. Serious dissension doesn't stand a chance – is crushed out of the majority before it catches on. The committed contrarians, they're the dangerous minority. The ones who blow the whole thing to pieces. Chloe, she's the quiet voice. The voice that can be ignored. Now and then she'll put something out there that's worth a listen, but it's rare: she's part of a generation with a lot to say but without the words to say it.

Not even a text to let me know what's happening. Maybe I should pull the plug on this one, call it a night and let her make it up to me. Christ, my throat is dry – I need refreshment. Fuck this, she can wait on me – if she turns up while I'm in search of liquid relief she can just fucking wait on me.

* * * *

Right, forty minutes now – forty! Pissy cunt. Maybe this is more than a Cosmo trick, maybe she's making a point about something. Women can be fucking bitches about the little stuff. Ok, I didn't say goodbye properly on Tuesday. So what? Can she really expect me to when she's bleating on about all this eco-shit? Trying to lay the blame on me for sticking this world and leaving it to rot? Don't put that on me, darling, you can go save the penguins if you like, but don't expect my heart to bleed for shit my granddad did.

Fuck sake, here she is – take your time, love. It's not like I've been waiting, drowning in the heavy beats of the drum and bass thumping from the speakers, clothes getting damper as the heat builds within me.

"Hey, babes," she says.

'Babes' – Jesus – the yanks have infiltrated. Even the counter-culture has been assimilated.

"Alright, love."

I'm not giving her an in here; she can make her fucking excuses, I'm not making this easy on her.

"Sorry, I had to help my dad get Mum up to bed."

And that's an excuse? Alright, if she'd spent twenty minutes getting ready I might have given her a break, but shit, same scruffy jeans, a baggy t-shirt, and fuck all make-up – yeah, she's made the effort.

"That's cool," I say, taking a sip of my too warm drink, "I haven't been waiting long."

* * * *

How big is too big? Eight inches? Ten, twelve, twenty? Ah, you're alright, pal, don't go shy. It doesn't matter what you're packing down there, you don't need to feel ashamed talking about it. The birds don't mind; you've got more to offer than your cock. Alright, I'm sure the dames would rather be sitting on a proper slab of meat like mine, but your teeny weeny ain't nothing to be down about. It's not all about length anyway, no matter what the meatheads tell you, no, girls are interested in a lot more than that. Girth, for starters. Oh yes, they like to get plugged by something with a bit of heft. Like to feel themselves filled up with heavy, swollen flesh – it's the ultimate reproductive fantasy, the throb of life pouring in and out. Women, they can't get enough, they ache for that fantasy. As I soon as I flop out the baby maker they can't wait to take it in, feel it swell and grow inside them.

Listen, don't believe the hype. Most women say they don't care, but they do. At least, they do when they meet a proper cock-slinger. You can see it in their faces. There was this skinny gint the other day – nice juicy ass – and things were heating up, were creeping towards the necessary. And then, all of a sudden, things went into turbo charge: my semi began to show and she knew what I was packing immediately. She couldn't wait to gobble on the magic stick then. It was straight to the bathroom, my friend; no questions asked. She barely said another two words before she was bent double, hanging on to the cistern and looking down at the skid-marked basin as I gave her both barrels. Oh yes, that's it, that's when you know. When they're creaming just to get a look; and when they lose their mind in the act. Simple. Bigger is always better, we've no time for small fry anymore – shape up or don't expect a whole lot of action.

* * * *

"Knobhead!"

I turn and watch as a lanky kid with greased hair makes his way down the street towards me.

"Jim – what's up, man?" I say, as we slap palms.

"Ah, nothing – where the fuck is everyone else?" He leans back against a wall, his angular frame emphasised as he stuffs his hands deep into his pockets. He's alright, Jimmy. He's green, but he'll flesh out like the rest of the world.

"Matty's almost here: he text to say he was on the bus like fifteen minutes ago."

"Nice," Jim says. His affected casualness creates a tension in the atmosphere, the awkwardness within him spilling out into the world. His limbs too long for his body, he packs them close to keep them from flailing. For a guy that takes up a lot of space, he doesn't take up a lot space. Funny that, presence being nothing to do with stature. See, a lot of guys get carried away wanting to pack on the muscle – become this great, Herculian beast – but they don't really get it; that's not how the world works. All those tumorous muscles popping out at every angle won't make you the centre of attention, won't give you that presence you desire.

It's about a whole lot more: we've evolved, you don't need to be able to crack rocks with your bare hands anymore, just handle yourself in the tangle.

"You heard from Smithy?" I ask.

"Nah," Jim comes back, "I ain't heard anything."

"Cool."

Smithy's a fucking liability of late: a freeloader. Lads aren't like girls; we don't need to be inside each other's pockets all the time, but you've gotta work for the whole a little. We're out here as free agents, but we're stronger as a unit, provided someone – fuck it, when I say 'someone', I mean me, – gives us some direction. Smithy needs to pull his weight, let his voice chime in.

"You see that girl he's nailing?" Jim asks.

"No," I say.

"Oh, mate, she is fit."

"Yeah?"

"Yeah. Seen her on his profile – she is banging."

"Where's she come from?" I ask.

"I would definitely hit that. Here…"

Jim loads the internet and hands me his phone. It snaps open straight onto a page showing a broad with layers of eye makeup on, peering up at the camera phone, which she wields above her own head. Eyes wide, she stares up into infinity, the camera looking past her gape and down to the cleavage that heaves upwards at the bottom of the shot.

"Nice," I say.

"Smithy's such a lucky prick."

"How old is she?" I ask.

"Dunno."

She looks about 14, but who's counting, right? If you can slip one in before they hit full bloom it doesn't do a lot of harm, and that bird is definitely up for it.

Jim's phone buzzes in my hand and Smithy's name appears on the screen. I take the call, "Hello."

Nothing.

"Hello?"

The hum of white noise subsides. I look down at the phone, 'Call failed'.

"Wanker."

I toss the phone back to Jim, irritated. The group isn't what it used to be – times gone by we were proper brothers – Project Mayhem – the lads, all out for a bit of the other, but in it together.

"Got a smoke?" I ask.

"Nah."

Checking my own pockets by instinct, I come up short. It's not a surprise, but still a disappointment. Life's made up of these periods of waiting on other people – you need something to anaesthetise yourself, something to give shape to the sludge of lost hours. Smokes are the perfect answer, the only answer that makes sense. Fiddling on his phone, Jim hasn't got a clue – it's something to kill the time, but it's passive, repetitive, draining. Smoking, that's an assertion, a positive. Smoking'll kill you. And that's the point. The creeping death comes to us all, and these periods of waiting – don't get it confused – these are what life is made up of. The bits that shimmer in between; they're

41

just illusory, they distract us from what existence actually amounts to. You've got to fight against this life, fill yourself up with shit that brings the end ever closer; that's how you take control, that's how you kick passivity to the curb.

"Look at the arse on her."

My eyes focus, look up at the street around me – nothing – then I turn to Jim, his arm outstretched, the glare of his phone's screen blinding me with an image of some girl jutting her bum out at the welcoming lens.

"Nice," I say.

"I'd have her," Jim confirms.

"Yeah."

A gasping rumble lets us know that a bus is dispatching its passengers just around the corner. Matty will surely be one of those stepping out of the grim interior and into the grimmer exterior.

"You looking to score tonight then?"

I turn back to Jim, "Sure. When aren't I looking to score?"

"True," he says, and goes back to flicking through social media, looking for t&a amongst friends of friends; enjoying the illusion of proximity, the added kick of reality that you don't get from porno. He hasn't woken up to the scale of the illusion yet – doesn't see the tiny box in front of him for the reality it is.

"Wankers!" Matty calls, laughing.

"Alright, Matty," Jim says.

"Easy, boys," Matty stalks over to us, his easy gait no more convincing than Jim's but his body in more comfortable proportions, "Where's Smithy?"

"Dunno," I shrug.

"So much for Project Mayhem – fuck me."

"You seen Smithy's new girl?" Jim asks, thrusting his phone in Matty's direction.

"Course I have – knocked one out over her on the way here."

"On the bus?"

"Not literally, you stupid fuck," Matty says, grabbing Jim in a headlock.

"Fuck Smithy; let's go," I say.

"Nah, he'll be here soon," Matty says, releasing Jim, whose body spreads out, limbs momentarily enjoying their freedom before clenching close to his body once more.

"You reckon?" Jim says, rubbing his neck.

"Yeah." Matty is calm.

"I'm sick of waiting," I say.

"Ten minutes?" Matty offers.

"Got a smoke?" I ask.

"Sure."

I take a tiny stick from the crumpled packet which Matty produces from his pocket. A burst of flame sets the tobacco alight.

We wait.

* * * *

I haven't had the horn for hours. It's always like this after a sexless hour in the sexless room, with sex completely off the table, out of the door and far, far away. Christ, it puts a downer on you. You've gotta work yourself right back into the world after that shit, turn things up to eleven and make sure you don't succumb.

I'll be alright, don't worry about me. I've got Lexi to look forward to tonight, eight o'clock and we're on. I've been waiting for it all week – a chance to work off some of the frustration. And it's on tonight, Lex has promised me something special, a treat – to say sorry for all the time she was off the map. I know her game, she's worried I'll go elsewhere, worried I'll take my prize pork and put it to better use. She'd hate that alright. Don't get me wrong, she's not insecure, not really: she knows I spread the love around but she's my number one girl – I've told her. She doesn't want that to change though, doesn't want to slide down the pecking order. After all, you never can rule out a trump card, a broad from left-field who blows the rest away, but right now, Lexi is my squeeze – I'm not going anywhere.

And boy, am I looking forward to tonight – a treat from Lex is a proper reason to get up in the morning. Last time she promised me something special it was a real mind-blower. See, I didn't know it was coming. Not what she had planned anyway. I was a bit mardy on her at the time because she'd not been paying me proper attention, had been jet-setting off around the world and not checked in like the good little girl she can be. So I was a bit cold to her. But this, well it melted everything.

Normally, when a girl says she's got a treat for you, they mean some new underwear (who needs it, right?

It's all window dressing). Not Lexi, oh no, brother, she goes the full way – she's pornography, your wet dream, the real deal.

So I'm sitting there, waiting for it all to kick off, when that hot piece comes slinking into the room, smooth black underwear keeping the conformity of her curves – the natural beauty that we all expect. Wet-lipped she pouted, stood hand on hip, knowing that her body spoke for her. But then this other broad came slinking in too. Some Yank chick named Anna – so Lexi introduced her, anyway. Her body was pneumatic, substantial, real. Christ, she dwarfed Lexi – not in size, but in stature. But Yanks, what can you do? It's a different world. Lex had picked well – she knows what I like, the feminine and the masculine rolled into one, the softness of the curves but the hardness of the soul. And this Anna, she was on the money.

I wanted to leap up and gather them both in my arms, smother them, own them, take them right there, but there was something in Lexi's face, something that said, "Sit there, big boy, enjoy the show." And, Christ, I did. Normally, I don't go in for all that breathy talk and soft, feminine faux-love. No, I like it real. But this little scene, well this was different. Lexi is different. She took Anna apart, sexually. Brought down the Yank aura, dismantled that stature, that superiority. She took her apart.

Jesus, that's what it's all about. Anna, she didn't see it coming. It's the sexual energy, the power; that's what we're in it for. It's not the physical, how could it be? It's the power, the domination, the unspoken submission to the cock. Anna didn't see it coming: Lexi, she was the cock.

* * * *

The fire exit door slams behind me as I stomp into the alley, a ball of energy, and crack my neck in anticipation. These are dangerous times – the world waits for the players to assemble, to take their place for the final scene of tonight's performance.

A grim-looking motherfucker in a leather jacket runs his eyes up and down me. He's a stereotype: shaved head, built for violence. This oaf could be on the door of any club, in any town. But he's not; he's here, sucking fags in neutral territory, no door to guard. Maybe there are enough blockheads to fill the demand, maybe there's no place left for these Neanderthals anymore, maybe it's amateur violence he's after.

The alley is clear, save for some grimy tramp huddled in his cardboard home, but this big beast waits on – maybe he's on a promise, maybe he's looking for some unlucky cunt to catch a beating. Well that's not me, pal. He can just keep his back pressed firmly against the cold bricks of the wall he guards – I'm the one on a promise here.

The door smacks against the wall behind me as it flies open once more; I turn, the hot fire of adrenaline sending dangerous energy through my muscles. Stomach-churning sickness sinks into my belly as my date drives his shoulder into my midriff, forcing me back against the wall.

The thick-set giant doesn't flinch as our furious tangle rages only inches from him; he just keeps sucking on his cigarette.

I bring my fists down on my partner's back, beat away as I feel him returning the favour to my sides. Striking down on his spine, his ribs, I just have to wait until something cracks: a bone, his resolve – I'm not picky.

The pressure of his hold soon slackens and he falls backs. With a swiftness reserved for agile fuckers like me, I bring my knee up hard and catch him across the jaw. His head snaps back and he goes down. It's done. I smile; look over to my solitary spectator. He raises an eyebrow half a millimetre, demanding more.

I turn back to my partner. He's still conscious, his pale blue hoodie now speckled with the blood that drips from his mouth. I swing my leg back and bring it through in a big kick, snapping into this schmuck's ribs. He jolts, then groans.

The lightweight tries to pull himself up to his elbows, but his head is foggy – he's out of his depth. I step back and take a run up this time – striding into the kick – and burying my laces deep into his cheek. He collapses down onto the welcoming concrete, littered with fag ends and takeaway boxes. I look up at our silent observer; he nods, a half-smile flickering across the lips still wrapped around his dwindling cigarette.

I grin back: I get it. He's a voyeur – an appreciator of violence, no longer a participant. His days are gone; our days are now. He looks on as I bury my foot in the now barely moving body on the floor. The kicks turn to stomps, but none are delivered with any real venom: it's all pantomime. My audience lights up another smoke, draws the toxins deep into his body. His eyes black under the light of the embers burning brightly before him, he looks on. He's resigned to his role – there's no spark, no twitch that says he's involved. This loser on the floor, he's barely a participant. It's his time, but he doesn't have the faculties to grasp it. I spit down on him as my leg grows weary from the effort, the fun dying as the short but gratifying gasps fail to come from the body on the floor. He's done before he's started; he's a different breed. Me, I'm the new wave, the fresh voice. I'm your dreams and your nightmares. I'm the thing you fear when you close your eyes and try to block out the reality of this world. I'm the end game, the final conclusion. I am the unstoppable force, the immovable object: I am Tyler Durden. I am the revolution.

* * * *

Fuck I hate mornings like these. Up late last night with Lexi (she only drops her panties when the blackness descends) – kept me at it for hours. Even after she was gone, everything was still electric; balls aching, cock raw, I lay awake thinking on things, unable to switch off. You know the feeling, right? But the morning after: always a bitch. Stomping pavements with my head throbbing every time my sole meets the solid ground. I should have stayed in bed. Wrapped myself up in the covers with a big mug of milky tea and my laptop; chased down some skirt or chatted to Chloe. That would have been the way to go. Still, I'm out now. Fresh and bright, the day lies ahead.

The distant rumble of a tube train tempts me, but it doesn't feel like a day to venture into the city, no, it's a day to ignite the brain, a day to go and check out the library MILFs. Oh yes, it's not all about the books down at our public service. Minge round every corner in le bibliothèque – if it's not the rebels skipping school, with their lips pierced and their school uniforms bulging with newly developed curves, then it's the horny librarians, rigid in their pastel cardigans, waiting for the opportunity to spring into action. You can tell they're up for it. All this repressed energy, see. They snap at the tiniest thing – a too-loud whisper, a book returned with the odd corner bent; defaced. When energy comes spilling out like that, you know they're just aching for the opportunity to really let it go. But touchy types, you've gotta fire them up, wind them up tight before you move in, offer that release, then boom. If you want a world-class blowjob, then get yourself an experienced librarian, my friend. Eager to please, intelligent; they understand the game, and they've all got that streak, that need to be part of the mainstream and outside of it, to go further than too far.

Clutching one solitary return to my chest I push on, Zarathustra resting close to my heart. These people wouldn't understand, as they go about their day-to-day lives, numbed to anything that matters; not an exception amongst them. They wouldn't give Friedrich a second look; wouldn't see the value. But then that's half his point, isn't it? These mundane, mediocre twats need someone who sees straight through all the bullshit, gets right to the heart of the problem. Man and Superman; Freddy knew his potatoes. He never followed it through though, never figured out how to put it all in place, how to get the lemmings to recognise their betters and accept a rational servility. But fuck them, everyone's out for themselves anyway, why should anyone get a leg up, a helping hand? Let the übermenschen cream the world of its riches and forget the ignorants.

The library is quiet today – alright, it's a library; it's quiet every day. Now, where to drop Friedrich? A couple of years ago, the library had these space-age pods dropped right in amongst the books; stick your items in and no need to speak to a human being in the process. The indifferent machines sit uncomfortably in the warmth of the converted barn where the local book collection has been housed for years. Ok, so in and out; bish, bash, bosh. Nice and simple you might be thinking. But don't forget why we're here: it's not all about book-learning and filling our heads with stuff, we need to get involved, get amongst it. I'm not shoving Friedrich into some anonymous bin for collection at an unspecified date; he deserves better. He deserves the warm embrace of a librarian, to have her finger run down his spine as she decides quite where she'd like him and if he belongs at all.

This one here will do. A little plain, possibly prim,

but a book-fondler no doubt. She'll do. She won't object, won't cause a stir and try to press me back into the machine's cold embrace. No, she'll accept my offering with a thin-lipped smile and beep it off my record without any issues.

* * * *

What a twat. Miss pastel cardigan. Miss 'You can't return a book in that state'. What state, love? Oh, a few bent corners, the odd stain. Jesus. Aren't books meant for enjoying? What a tight ass, anal cunt.

She thinks she can just turn me and Fred away? No recourse, no explanation. Fuck that. I'm smarter than your average: I'm not book smart, I'm street smart. She won't get one up on me. I won't bend over to be fisted by the system.

I've got a plan. There's always a way out. Sitting at this dusty corner table, part-hidden by a wall of books collected just for this purpose, I can see the cunt going about her business. Her tight, staccato movements as she mans her fortress. It's all so simple. She'll never see it coming. Take a pile of books up to be issued. Smile sweetly as she beeps out Auden and Amis (Kingsley, obviously), her heart fluttering a little as knowledge pours out of her range of control. Books issued, sit back at the desk and continue to 'read'. Nothing too amazing so far, but wait there, hold on just a second more. Give the bitch time to get on with her pathetic life and forget all about the fucking genius who's about to have her. Then, just before you leave, use one of the techno-pods. Haul that stack of books over to the returns kiosk, Freddy smuggled safely between Søren and Jean-Paul, and drop the whole lot into the unseen pit. Job done.

Before I get even though, I've got to look out a book on entrepreneurship. I've got a few plans, don't worry about that, my friend; something to top up the limp subsidy that wheezes into my bank account every fortnight. And while we're on it, JSA: Just Sucks Ass – who exactly can live on that sort of outlay? Alright, some of us have a roof over our heads no bother, but what about the lifestyle? What about the part of life worth living? Just get a job? You just get a fucking job, pal. It seems simple, doesn't it? With a fancy degree and spotless CV, oh yes, you can waltz into any tosser's office and demand a wage then, you greasy fuck. But that's not reality, that's not how it is on the ground. At the top, money just slops around, no rhyme or reason to it; down here you have to really earn it. No, worse than that; you have to earn the right to really earn it. Fuck. Most of these tight-ass employers don't even get past the paper – the limp CV, bald and apologetic – imagine if they got to me in person. Fuck yes, that'd be a laugh. Every now and then you slip through the net, the suits let you in, don't realise that you don't belong until it's too late, until you're on top of them.

But soon as you walk through the door they realise their mistake, realise that you're a live wire, someone who sees beyond. They don't want no part of you then, not when they see that look in your eye; that look that dares them to challenge you, to try and impose their reality on yours. Ha. No chance, mate. Tuck your dick in, polyester man, and waddle on because I'm not having any of it.

Interviews are difficult, see. When they take all that in, when you don't smile and collude in their pretence; you haven't got a hope. It's hard to know what frightens them more; that you acknowledge the pretence or that you dismiss it. Either way, you might as well turn heel and get the hell out of there as soon as they clock it.

But who needs the hassle of a job? I wouldn't mind some rightful employ; it'd be a distraction, and there are parts of it that appeal, but I've got better things to do with my time than join the bean-counting parade.

Employment: been there, done it. It's not for me, not right now. Not until something gives. So I'm stuck on this slap in the face, spit on your shoes pay out that barely covers the half. Sometimes it's hard to feel appreciated; sometimes it's like your contribution isn't valued. And let me tell you, anyone who does wretch out enough doe-eyed enthusiasm to find their way into a job soon regrets it. Down here work means work; they take your body and soul (they don't worry too much about the mind; it's not of value).

But don't get me wrong, I'm not against working; people do it every day. Sure, it's not the noble act that some try to make out, but it does. Well, it does for some. Others of us, we've got different priorities. We're just a little bit above, if you know what I mean. And listen, I'm not against money either, fuck, I'm out for all I can get. Eases the wheels, see, oils the shakes. Lexi might be bang on it, but when I get myself set up and in the money I could have a different girl every night of the week. Sure, Lexi'd still be my squeeze, but a bit of variety never hurt anyone. I reckon she'd get used to it. Besides, you can't go rationing what I got: everyone deserves a taste. But anyway, money, it's not all about pussy. Ha, who am I kidding? Course it's all about pussy. Money's only good for what it gets you: respect and blowjobs on tap.

This cunty librarian is still giving me the eye, sticking vigilantly to this end of her desk. She's knows the game's on, I'm sure. Knows Freddy is on his way back to her. Still, it's a bit much this: what does she think I'm going to pull? Eyeing me like I'm a criminal just because I'm on the rough-cut side of acceptable. Jesus. Meet me on the street, love. Try me out there; see how you feel then, whether you'd have the balls to keep this up in my library. We don't take prisoners out there; don't communicate through words or looks. This bird wouldn't have a chance; wouldn't even understand the language.

You've gotta feel sorry for people like that; so far off reality that they don't have any idea that they're adrift and beyond help.

* * * *

"You pissed?"

"What?"

Chloe looks up, confused.

"You look pissed," I say.

"Why would I be pissed?"

"I don't know – you look funny."

"Do I?"

"Yes."

"Well, I'm not angry."

I roll my eyes.

"No, you're pissed."

"Pissed?" she asks.

"Drunk on beer and alcohol," I clarify.

"I'm not."

"Well you should be."

"Are you 'pissed'?"

"No."

"Sure?"

"No."

* * * *

I breathe heavily as the toxic green beacon appears above the bump of the road, sticking proudly out from the grubby building: 'Job Centre Plus'. Plus what, I don't know – plus ball ache, plus demeaning, patronising shit, plus some cunt playing the social worker when he's about as qualified to help you find a job as a monkey in a tie.

Still, a little trip to the land of fake smiles and inept interrogations is hardly a high price to pay for your freedom. Slap on your best gear, fix a beaten-down expression on your face, and be prepared to explain how you'd love to get a job, it's just that it's so very hard, so very difficult out there. Fuckers. Most of them don't care really; they'll drink it in, sign you off, and bob's your hairy uncle, the dole-ars keep dropping into your bank account. Simple.

Oi, and don't go reckoning that I'm one of these pikeys either – one of those who flunks out of school at sixteen and spends the next forty years smoking fags and leeching off the rest of us. No, no, no, that's not me, your honour. I've got my grades – three A levels – and a fuckload more sense than most. Oh, and I've done the 9-to-5 too: mug's game. I didn't look back when they gave me redundancy. No chance. 'You're not redundant, the job's been made redundant', the soppy cunts tell you – no shit, brainiac; I reckon I'll cope.

Work is just a way to shackle you, to keep you in line. It's a scheme to give the masses a purpose, create the illusion that they're worth something. Well, some of us live outside those narrow rules, some of us choose authenticity.

Freedom – it's a beautiful thing – you should try it some time. Getting up with nowhere to be, no one to worry about what you're doing or not doing, just hours upon hours of freedom, stretching out before you, day after day. Beautiful.

Most people on the dole don't get it though; don't see how good we've all got it. These mopey cunts, who schlep in here bleating on about this cleaning gig, or that shelf-stacking job – fuck. It's not for me. Sure, you have to take yourself to the odd interview, show willing and that, but come on. Six hours throwing nukable slop onto supermarket shelves so that some buffalo-assed mong can sweep an armful into their trolley; enough to see them through another week. Yeah, I can think of better ways to live my life. I don't want any part of it, don't want to be responsible for feeding the obsessions of the masses.

They never see you on time at the Job Centre (Plus). No matter how late you turn up for an appointment, they leave you sitting in the waiting area, in one of the 'comfy' chairs, which carry every disease known to man, from syphilis to AIDS. It's a power play, so you don't forget that you're the lowest of the low, the dirt on the shoes of society. They can keep you waiting all day – you don't require immediate attention, are lucky to get even the mildest of pleasantries. So you sit and you wait, with the same greasy fucks you see every week, the same grubby tracksuits hanging off their scrawny frames, their feet shuffling in the same tired trainers – the laces frayed and the soles no longer a part of the whole, creeping towards detachment week on week. Scruffy bastards.

So they can leave me to wait out here all they want, because it does nothing for me. You won't go breaking my spirit; I look around and all I see is more proof that I am alone, that these are not people like me. I am above, beyond, apart, and oh so much better than these pathetic excuses for men. They need a kick up the ass, the lot of them.

So we sit. Sometimes someone breaks the silence – normally a new fucker – wants to communicate, connect. We soon put those soppy gits in their place. Quiet them down, let them know that we give less of a shit about them than we do about the fucker next to them. It doesn't take long before they fall into line.

Take this chipper cunt here, for example: check shirt poking out from his great woolly jumper. An alien. He's not on the dole, not really; he's just passing through. He's probably decided to take a sabbatical from the Law Firm and fancies a nice little sub while he swans around the Caribbean. Jammy cunt. He puts the rest on their guard, creates an uncomfortable tension. Knobless John – a true regular – is eyeing up this alien cunt's slip-ons. In another place, the posh nonce would be in for one. But this is the closest he'll ever get to reality – as soon as he hands over his national security number, he'll be gone: vamoose. Who can blame him? Away to the leggy wife and her welcoming bosom, which he shares with his own growing milk-sop. A long line of suckling pansies who drain the world of all colour and money. Good luck to them, but let me tell you, if you put those pricks in a room with me for ten minutes, I'd show them what it means to make the pig squeal.

The one tiny compensation for mingling with the dregs of society is the possibility of getting a half hour with one of the comely assistants: the ones who go through your current state of unemployability with you, who 'empathise' with your plight. So you wait, hoping for a Gemma or a Lily; a broad with big eyes and too much make-up, but who's yours for the duration.

No such luck today though; today it's Akbar at point C. Yep, this big-nosed, speccy cunt who's semi-retarded and less qualified to be here than I am. Jesus, where do they find these guys?

"So how are you doing today, John?"

Paki cunt can't even tell us apart – John, do I look like that dickless wanker? I hand him my CV and tap my name, written in bold at the very top, just like Gemma told me to do it last visit.

"This looks very good, very clean."

There's nothing on it, the fucker means. It's minimalism, it's uncluttered, it's the ultimate jerk-off.

"Thanks."

"Actually, last time you were in, Gemma organised an interview at the Shell garage on Townsend Street, yes?" Akbar says, looking at his screen and never in my direction.

"Yeah."

"And how did that go? Did they give you any feedback?"

Rejection is feedback enough, isn't it? How much clearer do you need it spelled out, you stupid prick? But it's not his fault: he's part of the old game, he's all in. He doesn't know I'm not taking part, that I'm not interested in reaching any sort of goal.

Play along, smile and assure them that everything's alright, that we're part of the same.

"No, not really. Said that I should ask more questions."

"Oh yes, you should definitely ask questions – appear engaged, you know? Prospective employers are always looking for someone who's interested in their business."

Appear engaged? Perhaps this cunt should polish his glasses, take a look beyond his flickering monitor and drink in the world that he's asking me to engage with. No, no, no, this speccy twat doesn't want me to engage. That wouldn't end well for either of us. I finger the handful of keys in my pocket, imagine raking one of them down this smarmy cunt's cheek and splitting it open, or thrusting it straight into his eye, bursting through to the soft flesh of the socket.

"I tried. I don't know a lot about petrol."

And I don't have any urge to find out either. No, you have to turn up to these things, but I'm not here to find a job, I'm here to have a life. It's best not to get into a conversation with these Job Centre people: if they begin to think you're interested, they'll 'go the extra mile', make sure you get a heads up on the best jobs first. You don't want to stand out like that, not with these pricks.

"Actually, there's a new call centre just outside town. They are looking for people at the moment; all the details are on the website," Akbar says. "If you look at one of the terminals you'll be able to apply." He gestures with his arm, pointing me towards a block of three computers by the wall. I look over, and then back at Akbar. His eyes are still fixed on the monitor in front of him: the cheap desk between us separates the apathy on both sides of the divide. I stand up.

"Cool."

The immigrant cunt smiles and hands back my CV.

"See you in two weeks, John."

* * * *

Urban parks: what a fucking joke. Tiny squares of 'green' dropped in amongst the great monuments to the City that burst from the ground all around us, reaching for the light and carrying their inhabitants further from salvation. But it's ok, we're not going to touch the parks; the space reserved for peace. Jesus, have you tried it - peace in this place? That isn't how we live now, there's only the frenetic pace; there is no slow lane.

The dopey secretaries with their soft, billowing skirts and tight woollen cardigans lounge on rugs while they eat their Deli sandwiches and flick through news items on their tablets. The simple life. The slick pricks in their sharp suits stride about, barking into their phones via Bluetooth headpieces, and slurping energy drinks to see them through another day. The secretaries look on – sedately, ironically – as these men of industry parade about, dripping with money but rarely any class. Are the women sold on the display, taken in by the rampant peacocking? Possibly. This is the only brand of men they know nowadays, these disinterested pseudo-cocks who occasionally throw a few crumbs out for the hens who peck around them.

It's easy for an insider to pick out the real cocks – these guys, they're not the same as me, but they still run the same game – I can size them up no problem. There's money on show today, no doubt, but no cocks.

Don't get me wrong, the two can mix, but it's rare, particularly in the trust fund brigade: cocks, they're the life force, the potent. They dominate. It's the new money, the rough money that's freshly polished, that's where you get the real deals. Patrick Bateman's the model cock: hard, unflappable, authentic. Not like these limp-dicked swaggerers. No – Bateman – he's the template, the ideal. Savagely modern, irrepressibly progressive.

Ok, he was flawed in ways. His personal grooming was a step too far; no one this side of bent needs to pay that much attention to themselves. A good hard body is enough, it does the job. Bateman, he over-complicated things by the end. And how he managed to end up hanging around with all those fags, I don't know. They would have been the first ones under the axe if I'd have been him; they're disposable. The whores, well, they have their repeat uses.

But listen, that's just being picky. Bateman, he had the right idea; weed out the trash and let the cream of society rise to the top. Me and Pat, we're unstoppable. It's evolution, it's selection of the fittest.

So why don't I wipe out these cunts right here? Follow them down one of the side streets and gut them? Well come on, you're smarter than that. Times have changed, cocks have finessed. I'm a little more savvy than that, don't you believe it. You've got to be, haven't you? Can't go round carving a path through life. These are the days for subtlety, for the steely undercurrent and the glossy exterior. So no, I'm not here for the suits.

I'm here for the hens.

This is a mission of lust, not a mission of war. It's time to give one of these girls a treat, to brighten their eyes before the afternoon dulls them with the computer-face-time it promises. Approaching girls in clusters like this – it takes balls, I'll grant you – it's not easy. But you gotta remember who you are and what you're offering. It doesn't matter how many of these other cunts gape as you disrupt their safe reality and pick out one of the flock. It's extra-reality, hyper-reality, their heads spin and their jaws drop. But you gotta ignore all that, it's not about them; they're jealous; confused; the ordinary.

So here's what you do – and don't go spreading this around the place, ok? – you chill out on the perimeter; try not to let any fucker clock you properly. That gives you the element of surprise when you do swoop in, see. It's less creepy, more natural, more spontaneous. So you scout the talent, keep an eye out for anything a little special: a bulging sweater smuggling heavy bazookas, the top of a stray thong that signals that its owner is up for it – you know the score, enjoy the buffet and take your time.

You'll find a good few targets any day of the week, so settle in, and see what comes your way. Right now there are three I've got an eye on: the redhead over there, with the tattoo down her arm – definitely a go'er; then there's that short dame on the bench – look at the rack on her! Norks as big as her head, I reckon; and the reserve, the blonde reading that chick-lit shit, bit of puppy fat, nice juicy hips. You can't leave it too long or they'll move on or notice you giving them the eye. You don't want that. Not really. You need to do a bit of observing first. What you want is a bird feeling a bit down on herself, someone looking for a bit of man flesh between her thighs. First thing you gotta look at is if they're clocking the men around them – they'll tell you they're 'people-watching', but they're not, they're scoping for a result like the rest of us. If you can catch one doing this a lot you know she's up for an interaction, open to being approached. That's an easy in, but it normally comes with the lower quality dames. Then you wanna look at how much she's checking her phone – if she's on it every five seconds she's too eager, or too involved in something else – that's no good. What you want is someone who is barely on the silicon, who's firmly planted in her surroundings, not distracted, but open to having her horizons broadened.

Red is skittering on and off her phone, barely stopping to shove wads of chicken wrap into her mouth. She's preoccupied, vacant. The busty dwarf is more promising, swinging her little legs and looking around the place. She might be waiting for someone, or she might be waiting for the big one. Blondie's dead to the world, reading her book and not here for the game. If I had to make a play, it'd be teeny, but you've gotta give it a few minutes, check she's not on a promise. So we wait.

Once the decision's made, it's simple: you walk by the target, casual like, take one pace past her and then stop, turn, and ask her something about her outfit or anything like that. Not in a camp way, and not in a pervy way. So for red you say, "Hey, cool tat," for the nerd, well, something about the book, and Busty McShortpants? That's a bit trickier; there's nothing obvious, and you've gotta stay away from the tits – whatever you do, don't comment on or eye up the tits. Enjoy them from afar, but up close you've gotta be more subtle, in the first instance. So maybe you stretch your back as you walk past, ask if she wouldn't mind if you shared the bench for a minute. Simple, see. The girls can respond to those approaches any way they want, but they can't be a bitch about it – you haven't pulled anything that allows it. In a club you'll get spat out all the time no matter how hot your shit is, but here the rules are different. You're using social convention against the drones – it's fucking awesome. Social convention says that they respond, that they're polite. And then you're in. It's so freaking simple, but it still takes more balls than you'd imagine. The real trick is to throw in the comment after you've almost passed your target – that's what makes it seem natural, and makes it seem like you're not planning to stay, like you have no real investment in the interaction.

Ok, so you throw out a simple comment. Get a little compliance; begin the unstoppable cycle of ever-increasing obedience to your will and to convention. You don't want to push this too hard too fast. So you half-smile at their answer, pause a second, ready to move on. You've gotta leave it to just the point where they're gonna look down, deflate their hopes – then bam, renew that hope afresh. And you don't have to be clever here: just say something. Don't get hung up on your opener, start afresh. Ask them where their accent is from. Better still, guess. Tell them they've got 'fuck-me' ankles – any old shit, they lap it up. Because at that point they're sold – it's hard-wired into them that they've got to put you at your ease, so if this is normal for you then they need to adapt. You're better off starting soft. When you're a swinging dick like me, you can pretty much run game from the off, walk right up and tell them you're going to fuck them until they moan and they can't walk straight anymore. Simple. For beginners though, you wanna be a little gentler, keep yourself within sight of accepted boundaries.

After you've got the conversation rolling, it's all about the close. Out here, that means a number or an online hook-up. In the club, it means a cab back to yours or a trip to the bathroom to abuse some boundaries.

So look, here's how you'd play it with smurfette. Straight past her, stop, hold your back, sit down. Simple. Once you're in, flip the interaction. Put it on her, point to a park shed and ask her if that's her office. Tell her you like her shoes, and saw a transvestite in a similar pair just the other night. Play her and smile while you do it. She'll be creaming for you in no time.

No change in proceedings so far, Blondie's put her book down, but our bench-dweller is still the best bet right now. Look at her, mussing the pleats of her skirt, heavy titties bulging out like a fucking invitation to touch. Shit.

Deep breath. Get the swagger on, kick your legs out

wide to show just how much heat you're packing down there. Oh, she sees it's on, looking up and then away. Coy bitch.

Halfway to the slut and I'm already at a semi – fuck, she is hot. I can feel the adrenaline kicking, that thrilling surge, that dangerous itch.

She's scratching her nail along the bench now, looking down as I walk past. Keep it up, love, there's no playing hard to get here.

* * * *

Want to know who's truly a cunt? Hey now, don't go coy on me, we're in this together – what's a little bit of language between friends? And don't go thinking you're better than me neither – sex and violence, that's what people want. You know it, I know it. That's what I deliver. Ok, maybe you don't want it thrust down your throat, maybe it's behind that respectable mask you wear, that hollow smile as you look out at the world through dulled eyes and ache for that thrill, that reality that you've only seen in films. Me and you, we're the same, pal. You might not have snorted crack and fucked a nameless stranger in a bar's toilet, might not have felt the warm swelling after you've thrust your head into the nose of some twat who's twice your size, but we are the same. We are all the same. Except we can't tell anyone, can we? Not even each other. Can you imagine? If we all let on, all realised that we were in this together? Fuck. Don't ever trust anyone who wants to 'understand you' – if they did, that'd be the end. Fuck Cosmo and fuck the fucking headshrinkers – they can all suck on my fucking dick.

Don't you come the amateur-psychologist with me either. You're on the level, I can see that. A little voyeurism never hurt anyone, but don't think this is anything more than that; the warm drip in your panties, that hard-on you're packing, that's all there is. You're not here to understand me. And why this obsession with understanding anyway? Shit exists, it is as it is, so get the on with it and stop intellectualising. That wall of vocabulary, all those clever words that separate us 'cultured', 'sophisticated' beings from our reality – it's all bullshit. This fucking pretence, it could all crumble in an instant. That day's not far off, my friend – be prepared. Those working class gorillas that make your heart flutter when the inevitable happens and you rub up against them - you poor, petted ponce - that keep you in your fancy clothes and warm, safe home – the line is that thin, my friend, that thin. You might say their day has been and gone, but I know, and you know, that that nagging doubt, that feeling in the back of your mind: It's real. It's valid. You should be afraid.

But look, maybe I'm jumping to conclusions. You're still here. You've not done a bunk just because a few cocks and fucks have been thrown about. So let me tell you about this cunt, and I do mean cunt. Annabel fucking Bird. Now she is one that thinks she's a cut above. If ever someone needed their eyes opening: the reality hasn't hit her yet. The inescapable and unalterable truth that her sex are finished, they've got as far as they can and the stark fact remains: men, we rule the world. So she can sit across the room from me, with her fucking notepad and blank, searching eyes, all innocence and concern, but let me tell you, I'd be doing her a favour if I ripped those sad M&S panties off and did a little 'exploring' of my own.

* * * *

A gleaming white bullet carries Lex across the Atlantic, off to the land of grubby dollars, drawling yokels, and fake living. It's all part of the lifestyle, all part of the job. Sex is a global brand, and Lex is a premium commodity. There's no denying that. No, the world want their fill, and who's she to deny them? She's the common body, the anomaly that we all deserve to enjoy.

Some limp dick tossers would be jealous, would be waiting up every night scared that some slab of American meat was slipping Lex the other. But come on now, that's not my style – I don't need to tell you that that shit doesn't touch me. Lex is free as a bird, good luck to her.

That Yank glean is long gone anyway; money, sex, power, it's gone global – no one has a monopoly on it anymore. The towering skyscrapers of New York had fallen long before the second plane; we all knew it. The twang of the Yank accent doesn't give girls that twinge these days, even the dollar sign is looking dated, its day long past. No, America doesn't have it anymore.

But then nowhere does. We don't chop the world

up by borders anymore, don't slice peoples and dice continents. It's all a sweltering mess, a fucking free-for-all. We went global centuries ago, today we've gone digital, and digital doesn't have borders.

See, that's the thing. Lexi might be thousands of miles away, but she's everywhere and anywhere I need her. Not even the necessary necessitates the physical these days. The air crackles with waves carrying human connection, linking us to one another, frying with the energy that it carries.

Fuck. That's liberation. A life without boundaries, borders, constraints. China are welcome to the world, because we've all moved on. The war's changed mediums and no one's fighting for the soil beneath our feet anymore.

So Lexi's fine, she's top. The Yanks can cut her as many looks as they want, but she's mine, wherever she lays her head. We're not exclusive, but ownership is a different matter, right?

Don't know how long she's gone either. Could be two weeks, maybe four. These things don't come with a structure from the outset. Tough on Lex, that. Hard to be out there schlepping around with all the greasy Yanks while you've got a cunt-busting package waiting for you back home. But she'll do her thing, smile her smiles and get through it. She's a pro.

* * * *

Things have stepped up a gear; it's all getting a little messy. I was chilling out with the tiny Kraut last night, nothing special, just kicking back, chilling, and she pulls some shit on me. We're happily chatting away, her banging on about some fucking whale that's being weeded out of existence or something, me trying to move her onto something a bit more interesting. I mean Jesus, whales – aren't there bigger problems to get hung up on? Anyway, she's spewing all this nonsense and then suddenly just stops, looks at me straight in the face. Shit, I hate all that. Sentimental bullshit. Moments straight out of tacky rom-com movies. Anyway, she looks at me all wide-eyed and serious, starts taking all these deep breaths as though she's about to fling herself into the abyss, then says, "You know I like you, right?" Fuck me – just comes right out with it like that. No pretence, no sub-text, just fucking throws it out there, straight in my face, no sugar-coating it or anything. I wanted to tell her that it isn't done that way. Wanted to explain that life doesn't work like the movies, you can't just put yourself out there and expect not to get ripped to shreds. Shit. And she just sat there, looking at me, waiting for a response. What do you say? How do you respond to that shit? Right then I just wanted to say, "Hey, tell me more about these whales," but fuck, that just wouldn't fly. So instead I sit there, trying to puzzle it out, trying to work out how to navigate this little problem.

And Jesus, she just sat there. Didn't offer me any sort of help, just stared at me, her dark eyes soft and fixed on mine. I couldn't take that shit, that soppy, hyped-up emotion; it doesn't have any place in our world, love.

Take that shit over to Yankland – they're all at it there, the fakeness of being 'real' and all that. Fuck. We don't do that stuff here, not with our dignity intact and all.

I couldn't keep looking at those eyes, had to drag mine away. I knew I had to come up with something, something to get us back to safety. I fixed my gaze on the Sonic Youth logo on her t-shirt, watching it stretch slightly as she took in ever deeper breaths, her tiny breasts pressing against the soft t-shirt. I wondered if she bothered with a bra, or if her ripe tits were free and loose under there, her nipples rubbing up against the cotton, just a little excited.

"Yeah?" I said, knowing full well it wasn't a proper response. I didn't look up though, didn't want any more of that emotional bullshit. I was happy where I was, fixed on those mosquito-bite tits, imagining what it would be like to sink my teeth into them.

She edged closer and I could tell she wanted some physical reassurance that she wasn't out there alone, that I was part of her conspiracy, that we were in it together. But I'm not a conspirator, I'm a lone wolf. She must have understood that. I've talked to her about Lexi a bit – ok, hadn't gone into full details, but she knows I like to put it about a bit. I don't know what she was hoping for, but as she edged closer I couldn't help imagining what it might be like. Not the romantic shit, I'm not into that: it's a non-starter. But the sack-game, how it would play out, whether it was worth a little investigation.

By this point, my crotch was aching, and even a naïve

twat like Chloe could see what was going on, could see the bulge that removed the burden of words. Her eyes really did widen then, when she realised what she had to play with, what I was all about. Her hands reached down to the hem of her t-shirt, clasping it with sweaty palms. I dragged my eyes up from her waist to her face, not sure what I was going to see, but risking it. Chloe gave me a questioning look and the faintest smile, hands poised and awaiting my instruction. I gave a small nod and dropped my eyes once more.

* * * *

Ever got a girl to squirt? Don't worry, pal – there's plenty who'll tell you it's a myth, that girls can't ejaculate. Bollocks, they all can – with the right guy in the driver's seat. It's not that hard, just a case of knowing the physiology. Most guys, they can't tell the vulva from the labia. It's the urethra that's the jackpot though, that's what it's all about when it comes to making them gush.

First off you've got to get her wet, not just the small trickle she'll get when she sees a real man ready for action, but properly drenched down there. You've gotta get amongst it, lap up those salty lips and give her a right seeing to. Your tongue's the only tool for the job.

If you've got to, go to the clitoris to get her cumming; work that bitch until she's ready to shit her pants with the pleasure. Then slip a finger or two inside and start working the G spot with a come-hither motion, driving her wild with your caresses. She'll soon be ready to blow, if you know half of what you're doing. Keep on her G spot until she's wild for it. Make sure you're teasing the clit too, and start working the urethra. Speed everything up a notch when she's ready to blow and spread your fingers wide so she can cum long and hard. Just make sure to put down some water-proof sheets before you set her off, because she'll make Niagara Falls look like a garden stream.

* * * *

Longest two minutes of the day. Get in, soles aching, mind grinding. I'm in want of a little relaxation, a little distraction.

Shoes off, I climb the stairs and drop down onto my bed, covers still falling into the inviting pool of my carpet where I left them this morning. Reaching up, I hit the power button on my laptop, which sits on my desk. Kim Kardashian appears briefly, then the familiar loading screen. Longest two minutes of the day.

I lie back on my bed; close my eyes and rest, wishing away the seconds until I have something to open my lids for once more. The computer's fan whizzes, the CD drive begins to spin – the familiar routine, the comforting commotion only inches from my ears.

I relax into the mattress, easing my hips down into the comfy groove, positioning myself so I don't have any springs pressing persistently on my spine. I consider where to start: a quick message to Lexi, letting her know how fucking hot last night was?; maybe open up my instant messenger and see who's online –

74

muff roulette?; or a sharpener? a quickie to one of my bookmarked scenes – the hot stuff, the shit?

The hard drive purrs and the fan begins to calm its agitated effort. A burst of chimes spring from the small but powerful speakers, telling me the seconds are passing faster than expected. I'll message Lexi first I think - it's only polite when she put on a show like the one I enjoyed last night. Damn, it's been a while, but popping that load was worth the wait – she gave me the full works, the slow build-up, the tease before the event. That girl knows how to treat a man.

The computer lets loose another chime, a double-take. I look up, concerned, but see Kardashian's famous bust right where it should be, the cursor spinning over her right nipple – teasing me and her at the same time. I begin composing the message in my head – it's got to be simple; appreciative, but not too much. It's not like Lex didn't enjoy herself last night – it was hardly all for my benefit, even if some stuck-up cunts might make you feel that way. No, she got both barrels, my wee Scotch lass. She knows how lucky she is.

The chimes fire across my thoughts again and I sit up a little, pulling the laptop onto my belly. The icons scatter across Kim's perfect body before my eyes, the cursor still spinning but more slowly now, easing off, preparing to draw the world into my bedroom. All looks fine, my heartbeat slows, and I rest back on my elbows as the final few programs load. Admiring those perfect caramel tits, hidden now by the mess of files dropped on top of them, I relax – but then the chime goes again. Shit. Maybe the sound card is busted; not the end of the world, but fuck scenes are less animal without the groans. And I certainly don't want any lovely to be competing with that dull chime, orgasmic screams being beaten out by the repetitive drone.

Time to reboot, relief further away than ever; three minutes until I'm hooked in once more. The screen dies, the tits disappear. The blackness grips me for a second, draws me in as though it has something to tell me. My whole body stops, muscles tingling with potential energy restrained. Then a tiny light - the bright luminous square of my phone's screen humming away next to me on the bed. My eyes focus, I look down at it: 'Josie', it tells me. 'Josie' is trying to connect with me. I accept the call and hit the power button on my laptop once more.

"Hello?"

"Are you home? Open the door, you knobhead."

The chimes start again, insistent. I blink at Kim's boobs before they disappear into another loading screen, brother to the one from five minutes past. I hang up the call and pull myself off the bed. As I trudge down the stairs, the chimes get louder and louder. I can see the dark shadow on the other side of the door, arm outstretched, finger held defiantly on the bell button.

I reach out, pull open the door; remove the distortion, give shape to the shadow.

"Hi, Mum."

"Lazy sod - you think I want to stand out here all day with the shopping? Give me a hand with these."

I reach down and pick up the abandoned plastic bags, the carefully stacked boxes within slipping and spilling, order no longer kept.

* * * *

It's one of those evenings. All I want is to escape to the real world, but instead I'm stuck with the mundane. Alright, I wasn't on it earlier. Fair play, no one wants to be left hanging, although, let's be honest, if Mum had remembered her key she wouldn't have been stood out there, waiting. Not like her either, forgetting the basics. Didn't stop her from having a strop, making me stack some cans and fill the freezer with her haul. She knows I don't like all that domestic stuff. Knows it gets right up my nose. Dad wouldn't have put up with that shit. Fuck, Dad *didn't* put up with that shit. The nagging, the bitching. He's well off out of it.

But I'm here, so I did my bit, held my tongue, played the little darling. Once I'd emptied the bags, flung the stuff into a cupboard, you'd think that would be it. Normally that would do. Not tonight.

Soon as the stuff was put away, she was straight on the sofa, TV on, tea in hand. Fuck, makes you laugh. That people can spend their lives staring at the box, pretending it's a two-way medium, that they're doing anything but filling time before the end, disguising the silence, dulling the senses. So had her bleating on about her back, how it aches and hurts, for ages. Jesus, what am I, the social? I don't need any of that shit. You don't have to convince me, the benefit cheques keep coming whether I'm in on the act or not.

So it's 'fend for yourself, kid – I'm all right, Jack', 'I'm not cooking, lad.' Fuck. Takeaway's out of the question. We're too far from the heady rush of benefits day for that. We're onto scraps, onto the dregs.

So it's down to me. Packets ripped open, cans unburdened. Slap the mess into the microwave and nuke the shit out of it.

She just sits there of course, watching that shiny poof on the telly. Christ, if that isn't a face you'd slap. I'm no homophobe, but Jesus, wouldn't you? Smug twat. And look, I don't mind what he gets up to in his private life, so long as he doesn't go bothering proper cock-slingers like me. It's fucking disgusting, but hey, no accounting, right? If he'd rather fiddle with some burly bloke's cock than finger the minge, then all the more for the rest of us, right? This guy though, no disrespect, is a wanker. Why Mum doesn't put on some nice bird to tell her about panty-liners and liposuction, I don't know.

* * * *

Dinner drags. Mum and I feet apart but separated by the shit that comes out of the box. She picks and prods at her food, as though my cooking isn't up to scratch, as though I don't know how to use a fucking microwave. It's painful. I just shove mine down: no point messing around. So I wait; for dessert, for a resolution to the food-chasing game she's playing around her plate.

This is how it goes some nights, sucked into the torpid drudge that is 'real' life. I mean Jesus, why bother? You might as well stick your head in the oven. At least I've got life outside these four walls, at least the moving pictures don't represent the most involving part of my life. Mum didn't used to be like this, but then who did? When Dad was around she was up and firing, always attacking him for some shit. At least she had a bit of life force then, at least she registered her existence on the scale. Now look at her. Swilling mush that was once food and counting down the days. Ok, she tarts herself up on a Thursday for the Social Club. Goes down there, bright-eyed and looking for the 'one' or a good shag at least. But she knows – we all know – that isn't how it works anymore. The odds just aren't in your favour. So we continue on like this, existing.

I'm with Dad really, he knew when to get shot, when to seek out something a little more than the ordinary. He's like me: restless energy, and he likes the birds. It's where I get it from. Ok, I'm the new breed, a little more class than a fumble in the back of a van. That's how it goes though, right? The new replaces the old; we evolve, improve on previous models. Dad, he was rough around the edges. I'm in high-def, in three gleaming dimensions. He'd be proud, he'd see a lot in me.

* * * *

Back to the boudoir, back to my lair. Mum's not so bad, happy as Larry down there, watching her programmes. She knows her place in the grand order, I suppose: the mother provider, woman's lot. She's done her thing, kept the species moving forward, and now it's time to settle back and let nature take its course, let those of us who are up for the fight flourish.

* * * *

Who writes these fucking lists? "The 100 Hottest Women on the Planet!" Jesus, how do you ever get it down to one hundred – even if you only include the dames lucky enough to fill our glossies and our minds.

Now, it's a cracking job and it's a worthwhile cause, but really, how do these guys go about it? There's some serious misjudgements if you ask me, and I know what I'm talking about. When you flick across the various lists, there's no true conclusion, no complete coverage. The whole thing is a long way from scientific, a long way from democratic, even.

If it was down to me, there'd be a much better system. First off, there'd be some quantifiable way of sorting women. Easy now, we all do this, don't go pretending you're above it any more than the rest of us. What's your tipple? A great heaving rump, maybe taut abs? Perhaps you're less discriminating; perhaps you're from the days when gentlemen preferred blondes or brunettes – that was it, the whole criteria?

Well these are the new days, pal, we're a little more discerning, a little more demanding. Me, I've got my predilections. Course, I'm happy to bend the criteria for a tight little honey even if she falls outside the normal. After all, when it comes down to it, you vote with your cock, don't you? A thumbs up is a thumbs up.

You've gotta have an ideal though, haven't you? The

ultimate fantasy, the perfectly pornographic. I like 'em big on top, but I'm not telling you anything shocking there, am I? Skinny waist is a must, and a pierced navel sets off tight abs. A smooth bum, round but not flabby. 5'4"-5'7", dress size 8-10, although I could go down to a 6 provided she still fills a bra out. For the face – that's still the vital, right? – I've gotta have the hint of freckles, and proper bone structure. Not too harsh, but defined. Blue-green eyes, made up with thick black eye liner and lips that pout proudly. Voluptuous hair, dark brown and curvy. That's a woman, my friend. That's how it ought to go.

I'm no fool, though. Everyone has their own little wants and fetishes. So here's the thing: why don't the guys who compile these lists get all this information together? Poll us guys out here – the ones who actually have a clue about what's desirable, and then put the results together and see which women match up best. Simple. You'd have a top 100 then, my friend. That'd be real objectivity. You know, you could even break it into categories: Best Tits; Best Arse; Best Lips, and so on. That'd be a good read, a true guide to who's packing what.

I'd put Lex up against any of the dames on the lists at the moment – she'd blow them out the water; they just wouldn't have a chance. But it's the impossible dream: she's outside of the mainstream, not a clone but a cracking of the model. These lists, they're for the safe middle ground.

* * * *

Wouldn't you love to have some pliers to hand just now? Clacking her teeth together, breaking the silence while she stares me out. Good luck, love, I'm not showing; we can just sit here for as long as you like, dear. You just go on clacking those caffeine-stained chompers; see how far that gets you before we try a little amateur dentistry.

I don't answer questions: that's not how this game works. So she can just sit there in her cheap, shiny trousers. Scuzzy dyke. Let me tell you something, this Annabel Bird is a fucking cunt, make no mistake. She'll pretend that she's trying to help, that she gives even half a crap. Ha, no one pulls that shit on me. This is professional, we both know it. One hour a week in some grubby block out back of the hospital doesn't add up to a caring relationship now does it? We're on the clock, always.

And talking of the old psycho-babble, well, this bird is one anal cunt. Yeah, I know all that Freud shit. And, no, I don't want to shag my mum, but you've gotta know the landscape, haven't you? You can't just walk in to this sort of thing blind – they'd make short work of you. You gotta protect yourself against that shit, close your mind off from the brain scrapers.

So yeah, I'm up on the game, I've read all those dirty old Jews and their ideas about what I want to do with my cock. Jesus, did they ever think this racket would work? 'The talking therapy' – it's a joke, right? They charge people to have their problems 'listened' to, then sit there, like a comatose twat, and have the balls to tell you they've helped you. Oh, it's quite a gig, my friend, but people lap that shit up. They can't wait to fling their money at these con artists, can't wait to drop their grubby notes for some human connection, some intimacy – the saps. And let me tell you, trading in a commodity as common as intimacy is nothing new – women have been doing that since they first realised the value of their sex. There's always someone willing to pay, except now they don't even drop their knickers. Annabel Bird isn't selling one ounce of herself; not a single heartbeat of her existence is wasted on the clientele. No, no, no, this is the new age; even the whores don't empathise anymore.

But you know what? That's fine by me, because I'm not buying. Not from this twat, not from any twat. This man is an island, and I'm not in a hurry to crack out the dingy and go exploring foreign waters. I'm quite happy here in my paradise; I've got everything I need.

* * * *

I close my eyes: the comforting whirr kicks in beside me, the quiet commotion of fans and drives awakening, ready to offer the escape we all desire. The familiar chimes sound and I open my eyes to let the bright images in; almost there, almost plugged in once more.

I blink over at my clock: 06:58am. Awake early with nowhere and everywhere to be. For the majority, sleep is just part of the daily pattern, for those of us who opt out of the routine of life, sleep is the only thing that offers shape to the day. We take it when we want it, not when we have to. It's a freedom most people don't appreciate – the ability to decide when to rest and when to play.

I look back to the screen, the laptop well into its stride now. Opening a browser, I watch as the icons splattered across the desktop disappear to be replaced by a white screen and a blinking cursor: a search box. The aching void, pregnant with possibility and blinding in its sparseness, stares me in the face.

We can't handle absence anymore, anything is better than the blankness; the quiet of nothingness. People fight to put images of love and hate – both equally nauseating – between themselves and the blank space that surrounds us. It's the only escape, and yet we feel the pressure of the blankness pressing in against us, forcing the violent display ever closer, forcing us to demand images brighter, more graphic until they scorch our senses badly enough that we no longer feel the void and the images become our reality.

But it's ok. Most people don't need to fear absence anymore – we're blinded, permanently. There's no need to seek out the light show that protects us either; inoculation precedes the sickness now. Sedation isn't an option, it's a shared reality. Most people don't see the beauty of the system, how perfect our salvation is.

My fingers ache and my eyes burn, the bright white too much in the still-dark room. I blink, and my fingers scuttle across the keys: 'Perfect teen body'. Words flash onto the screen, links taking me off in different directions, narrowing my options at each click, only to offer new possibilities within a few seconds. The words swim, and I flick to image results: the softness of form far gentler than the erect definiteness of language. Peach bodies blur across the screen, and I focus, picking out the details amongst the mass: anorexic girls in bikinis, Baltic muscle boys. In focus all is hard; bones, sinew – all proudly displayed.

My chest tightens and I open a fresh window, call up a news site.

I click back to the wall of hard humanity and search again: 'Soft teen girls with big curves'. The news flashes for my attention and I respond. As my eyes dart across the headlines, the words cut only so deep. Wars, murder, scandal. I search for a date amongst the articles, to verify that this is today's news, that it's not a regurgitation of yesterday's or the day before's.

Fresh bodies fill my senses. This time the hardness is hidden beneath soft flesh, disguising the fragile bones beneath. I breathe easy, the pillowy comfort of this new selection exactly what's needed for this time of the morning. I run my tongue over my bottom lip, the rough dryness of my skin softened as the warmth of my tongue moistens all.

I click onto a particularly promising image. The big eyes, staring down the camera's lens, draw me in, insist that I engage with this body, remote from my own. The new page loads, and more bodies appear, contorted but vital. All screaming for attention but knowing that no gaze will linger on them for more than a few moments.

The headline tells me these bodies are now lifeless, fallen to a regime who no longer values them. I pause, but fail to see the vitality fall from their eyes. I refuse to read beyond the headline – news is all propaganda for some cause or other, no one is motiveless.

I scan for total nudity – why stop half-way to anywhere? – and pick out a few choice cuts of meat. The robustness of the female body, the power to populate and titillate, is overwhelming at its bloom. The innocence of heavy hips is liberating, and these chicks are all for liberation. It's real teens we want here, fresh from the violence of puberty. You can skip the aging wannabes, their hair in pigtails and baby pink blusher on their cheeks. Look for the gawky, the suspicious; they're the real deal. You'll only find a handful on any page, but they're worth the price of admission. I take my choice and narrow my options. A round, vulnerable body fills the screen, unmanicured and impossibly potent. Blood rushes and I am afraid.

I lock eyes but see no flicker of humanity. Out of shot, bullets fly and bodies fall. In shot, there is only death. War is forced upon these people, and they take up arms naïvely. They fight for a cause, but die for another. Wars are fucked but they'll never stop, the sums are pretty simple: wars are good for most people with power and bad for most people without. Arms dealers, politicians, big business; they profit from conflict. The average man's only interest is a moral one. And so it's the moral man who fights, who stands righteously on the frontline while bullets fill bank accounts, and images of heroism and death are captured and sent home to remind the rest of us – the amoral cheerleaders – that we're still alive.

Ripe flesh burns through your consciousness. There's no connection but there's the prick of knowledge, of reality. The violence of the human form scares and intimidates, vitality as fearful as flaccidity. The only sign of life, the blood that rushes from my brain to my balls, firing the inevitable and leaving me sick with lust for the intangible; my hand reaches out for soulless pleasure and grasps firm flesh.

* * * *

The murmur of a thousand voices, shrill tones bursting out from the crowd occasionally. This is what people do on the weekends: pile into plush shopping centres to gape at objects they don't need, can't afford, and barely believe they like.

As they swarm about in tiny clusters, it's clear that fun is off the agenda. Children scream, couples bicker, and no one smiles. The hum of activity disguises the reality, but if you stop, take a moment to breathe amongst the activity, the truth of the situation bears down on you. The air of dissatisfaction is thick; and this is what people work for, this is how they choose to spend their free time.

I rest my hands on the rail of the middle concourse, lean over, and look down at the layers of artificiality – floor upon floor of shops. An ant's nest, but without purpose. I sigh, scan the masses for any likely targets, any girls worth heading towards. There's little on show. Velour tracksuits and fraying leggings disguise bodies, good or bad.

I stand, catch the metallic smell my hands have inherited from the rail, and turn, ready to begin the rounds. With drudgery everywhere, it's not hard to offer that spark of something different, to be the person that makes the trip to the shopping centre worthwhile for someone else.

Girls hunt in packs in closed environments like this, or with their boyfriends – these social creatures aren't worth the effort. You've got to be smart, look for the ones hanging out in front of clothes shops, looking longingly in as though they might belong, possibly, if they could just shed those few pounds, just get their skin clear. Those are the ones.

There are a lot of couples today: too many to make it comfortable for a predator like me. Sure, a marked woman can offer a bit of eye candy, but that's about it. There's no end game, it's all a tease. Girls look at couples and want what they have, men look at individual women and want to fuck them. It's just how it goes. Standing here, watching people go by, I'm not happy for any one of them, not jealous of the guys with dames on their arms. No, I look and I desire. I undress the girls, peel the layers from their bodies with my eyes. Clothes are the root of all unfaithfulness. They create the illusion, the lie, beneath which all possibilities lay. Guys, we can't help ourselves: curiosity must be gratified and so you're in a constant state of aroused temptation. If everyone just lived naked and free we'd soon see how few alternatives there really are, would soon settle without going looking for an upgrade, scoping for a fresh result.

Making a swift turn to the right, I stop at the juice bar. The place is staffed by girls with tight-fitting and brightly coloured t-shirts, their pneumatic bodies alive with vitality. It's the ripe, the prime that serve in places like this: they're the perfect advert for the product. A succulent sort sways my way:

"What can I get for you?" She brushes her hair away, runs her eyes across me.

"What do you suggest?" I smile.

She smiles back, "The citric burst is really good."

I look up at the board above her. "Sure."

She begins to grab the fruit from its bowl, chopping and chucking it into a huge blender. She smiles over at me again. Definitely interested.

"That t-shirt's a bit bright, innit?" I nod at the fluorescent, lime-green tee.

"You don't like it?" She pulls it down at the hem, surveying it.

"Doesn't it hurt your eyes?"

She laughs. I laugh. We're good.

The violence of the blender disturbs the atmosphere, shredding flesh and liquefying its contents.

As suddenly as it erupted, it falls silent.

The girl places the cup carefully on the counter.

"Looks good," I say.

"Delicious," she says. "That's three-fifty."

I count out the change, continue to flick between sly grins and disinterest; the perfect balance. She looks on, smiling.

Counting slowly, I push the coins across the counter. My hand brushes hers as she retrieves the plunder and I feel the tension in her touch. She wants it.

"Thank you," she says, and hands me the receipt.

"See you again," I grin.

A good interaction. Enough to get loose, and put a little shot in her coco.

Sipping on the citrus drink, I look around. Everywhere, wannabe wags flounce up and down, their hair bouncing and hips swaying as though they're on the catwalk; the muscle lads pissing about, showing out; those on the outside, the average, their jaws gently dropping as they gape up at the unobtainable beauty in the shop windows. It's a fucked up world. We used to teach people to lower their expectations for life, now we teach them to shoot for the moon. Half the world feel like they're on the cusp of perfection, the centre of the universe. The other half are desperate, falling to the impossible dream, gawking at the glamorous reality that's thrust in their faces.

This is the reality they create for the dull twats who can't develop a personality for themselves. Don't get it wrong, this is the majority. We don't have interests anymore, don't have personalities. This corporate world would never allow it. And we're the great individualistic West. Maybe we should all go red. Collectivism can't be worse than this shit. At least then you don't have the illusion of freedom; the power to dream an impossible dream. The Russians and the Chinks have it right. Each one of them know from birth that they're nothing special, that no one's looking down on them, promising that they're different, a cut above. Regular cunts, they need to get used to the idea. You can't do anything of your own volition anymore. If something's worth doing it's appropriated, becomes part of the whole: commercialised, shared, generic.

Girls giggle as they pass, snapping away on their camera phones, documenting everything: a look, a fall, the world through a lens. We capture everything for posterity – images, films – store it away, document a life that's of no interest to the rest of humanity. Perhaps it helps maintain the illusion that you matter, you sad prick. Perhaps it makes you feel that the story of your life is worth telling, that you'll leave some sort of trace in this world, you delusional bastard.

I drift towards the bakery, drawn towards the smell of roasting meat cocooned in warm pastry. Some noisy Pakis in saris try to walk straight into my path as I cut across stream, but I just keep on in my own direction – scatter the heard. These foreigners – they don't play by the same rules we do. You've gotta educate them in first-world manners. I press on, tossing the empty juice cup into a bin overflowing with the remnants of 'stuff'.

The lad in the baker's is a right chunky fucker – he fits the bill, surrounded by pork pies, chicken bakes; he's found his place in the world.

"Sausage roll." I point down to the freshest of a poor

selection.

"That's one ninety-nine. Would you like anything else?" he says, as he rings the price through the till. The drone of the printer as it coughs out a receipt has more range than the flat drawl of the cashier's voice, the life force more vital in machine than man.

I pocket the change and stalk out – the warmth of the sausage roll comforting after the coolness of the juice. High-pitched screams let me know that more girls are on the prowl, but when I turn it's some fag making all the noise, surrounded by fawning girls, delighted by the novelty of their 'gay friend'. Fucking fag hags; they're the total pits. They snap their fingers and sass their way through life, believing they're being independent, that they're living the life authentic. Stupid whores. If they could clap eyes on themselves they'd see what a bunch of dolled up slappers they really are, screeching away, thinking they're worth something more than nothing.

The noise overwhelms. Not just the fag hags but the full orchestra; the screaming kids, lads growling in packs, doors slamming, sliding, tills crashing, phones blaring. Already invisible to the world, I close my eyes. The noise crashes in and I surrender, let reality slide and darkness take over–

* * * *

The mushroom cloud is the daddy of all televisual experiences – the bulbous, burning smoke that signalled the age of anxiety, of imminent death as the only reality. The liberal dickweeds moan and fret about the power of the atom, but it's liberation, my friend. They need to wake up to the fact. The burning dread of death, it's the only thing that keeps people alive. Making that fear ubiquitous is the best thing the Yanks ever did for this world.

Today fear has receded – toddled off to the corner of our consciousness where it's quietly thumbing its breeches, waiting for an opportunity to pipe up once more, to remind everyone that it's still the force in these parts. For a flash, the new generation thought its moment had come – thought fear was back in the game, alive and well. As smoke billowed from the twin towers, there was an intake of breath as the world prepared to welcome fear back into the fold.

But Osama's little orchestration could never match Oppenheimer's – if there's one thing the Yank's know how to do, it's put on a good show. Sure, fear started limbering up for its first appearance of the new millennium – its triumphant comeback tour – but it just didn't have the legs anymore. The world is too full of images to allow one to rise above the rest these days, so back into its corner fear went, tail between its legs. We don't need that shit anymore – fear is on the side-lines, an ever-present but no longer a key player in the true game.

* * * *

The internet is the fucking shit. No matter what you want to see, bang in a few words and it's there – you're never more than five seconds from full satisfaction. How did guys ever survive before the www. revolution? How did they deal with women when all they really wanted was a flash show? See, that's why women today have a much better deal of it. Fuck, listening to some of those bra-burning types you'd never guess it, but they've got it made right now. Every guy from the age of thirteen upwards can log on and crack one off no bother, perfect bodies writhing in any arrangement you like. We get all that carnal shit out the way in cyberspace where no one blinks, no matter what our predilections are. And let's be honest, we like it hard and dirty. No one, with the whole world at their fingertips, searches out the soft-tone, sweet stuff. We all go for the tight dame being gang-banged by seventeen ex-soviet meatheads who slap her body around all over the place. That's the shit, that's what we want. And that's why broads today have got it easy. We don't expect that shit from them. Years ago, you'd have guys packing full on erections for years at a time, scrabbling round trying to find a good shag, desperately trying to unload. Jesus, pity the virgin that winds up on the end of that.

It adds up, doesn't it? You wouldn't think so, not listening to the whole 'objectifying women' brigade. Fuck, just because they're frigid doesn't mean every cunt is. If some broads get off on the hot stuff and earn a dime in the process, where's the harm? It's all good, clean fun – right? Course, they won't let anyone believe that, have to keep pushing to make sure everyone feels guilty about enjoying life. Well, not me, I'm not up for that shit – I love pussy and I've got no problem enjoying it, however it comes.

Look, the world really is your oyster now, and it's all no strings, no hassle. Most times I'm into the curvy girls, really young and stacked. But some days, today being one of those days, I want something a little different. Today it's the scrawny type I want, the type you can imagine throwing around the place, bouncing her off the walls and letting her know who the daddy is.

Skinny sluts with no tits might not be the mainstream, but there's the odd 31,000,000 (approximately) for me to work through right now. Shit, who has time for all that? You'd be lucky to find many guys who can get through 0.01% of that stuff before popping their load – alright, I might be the exception, might hang around a little longer, but even a primo meat packer like me wouldn't see the other side of 1%. That's a whole lot of sluts going unappreciated, their dignity sacrificed for all but nothing.

Talk about competition, this is it right here: millions of girls ready to open themselves to you, and with a few keystrokes you view and dismiss them. This is the world, this is how it works, my friend. It's raw but it's true, none of this pissing around with the farm girl up the road, dancing the dance for a barely worth it treat: a chaste kiss, a year-long tease. Chastity doesn't work as a model anymore. We're past that, it's not an option. No, this is what it's all about: log on and filter out. It's evolution at its finest, survival of the fittest and all that. Shit, see half these girls on the street pre-net days and you'd have been on it quicker than blinking, but lay them out here and most won't even raise a semi.

See, Chloe doesn't have a chance here. A few careful keywords and I've upgraded – Chloe 2.0, fuck it, Chloe 10.0. Skinny, black haired chicks splurt across my screen, thighs lacking even a hint of cellulite, tits a bit perkier than the Kraut's, stomachs a little flatter. Take your pick; it's all here for you. Your average girls, they don't stand a chance. Not with a guy like me, not when I know the full extent of my options. This is what those ear-benders are really worried about. They can wrap it up in clever theories and complicated arguments all they want, but this is the truth, this is what they fear: a world where we all have a choice. Because if you have a choice, there's always a chance you won't choose them.

* * * *

Ramona. A beautiful Mediterranean name, it rolls off the tongue, conjures up images of a sultry, pouting broad with tanned limbs and dark eyes. Ra-moan-a. It's sexual, its carrier obliged to fit the ideal that it promises.

I ease my oversized cup around the saucer on its edge, the grating of china irritating just the slightest. Around me, posers chatter and the smell of coffee intoxicates. The furniture every shade of coffee brown, I'm surrounded, disgusted, while I wait for this Ramona. Coffee shops, they're the quintessential sparring ground for new relationships. Where nervous teens and geeky guys take their squeezes to impress them by how modern they are. It's total bullshit. It's the artifice of a life that's desired only in theory. Given half the chance, I'd have settled on somewhere a little tighter. But Ramona, she was all for a 'relaxed', 'public' place. Dozy mare – what does she think is going to happen here?

Relaxing into the comfortable seat, I fix my gaze firmly on the door, waiting for that spark of recognition from one of the people who file in. Ramona and I, we're in the same position – nothing but an avatar to go on, but she'll know me, there's nothing false about my identity. Her, well, we'll wait and see. Headshots are bullshit – from the neck down she could be a bloated binge eater, or a flat-chested man impersonator. It's a gamble. But it's ok – that's half the fun. If she's sub-8 on the hotness scale, I'll be out of here before she's had a chance to down a skinny latte.

The door rattles open, allowing a burst of sound from outside to infiltrate the chatter within. A skinny bird in a long skirt and vest top steps in. Hair down to her waist, she's festooned with all manner of scruffy bracelet and trinket. Fucking hippy dyke.

I run my eyes over her, and wonder if she's the one. Eyes look about right, although the skin is punctured and pock-marked far more than in her profile, the eyebrows bushier, the teeth goofier. We lock eyes and, giving me a half-smile, she begins to make her way over. Shit.

Stopping short, she stands by the chair opposite mine and offers her hand.

"Hi, I'm Ramona."

There's a question in her voice, and I nod in answer. Her palm is sweaty as we shake, and I notice the thick black hair running down her forearm and snaking onto the tip of her wrist. Something in me wants to heave. Hairy girls, no, they're not the modern. Imagine the bush on this little cave girl; if she thinks it's ok to glide around with all that going on in the open, I don't want to find out what forest she's hiding away in her panties.

I feel bile rise at the back of my throat and grudgingly I get to my feet.

"Hi," I say.

Standing face-to-face, I evaluate: decent bone structure, everything in the right place, but the skin; try some fucking Clearasil, love. I look for the pouting lips her name promises, but find only limp flesh pressed outwards by protruding teeth. Above her top lip a thin row of hairs point down to the orifice below.

The feeling of sickness grows, and I can't help but imagine what thick matted tangle lives in this Ramona's armpits, what percentage of her body is coated in fine, dark hair, covering her like a poorly evolved version of the rest of us. For a moment, I fixate on her belly and imagine what lies beneath. My stomach turns and I'm sure I'm going to heave.

"I'm sorry," I say.

She looks confused, but I continue, pulling my phone from my pocket and brandishing it by way of explanation.

"My Mum – I have to go."

I push past the mini-yeti, who doesn't move for a

moment.

As I press through the door, I feel a hand on my wrist. I turn and see that the yeti is no longer frozen in time, that she has followed me through the door and out of the coffee shop.

"Is something wrong?" she asks, concerned.

I look into the deep black eyes as we stand facing one another in the street. A greasy fuck in a suit power walks straight towards us, his mobile phone pressed to his ear, and we step to one side, making way for the constant stream of people who chase their next caffeine hit.

"No," I say. "I mean, Mum just called before you came and said she wanted me home. I don't know."

There's a sadness in Ramona, leaking from her eyes.

"Is it something I did?" she asks.

They're all the same – women – all want to turn things round to themselves. It's the only way they can cope with the world, only way it makes sense to them.

"No," I say. I stare at the ground, the grey of the cracked paving stones easier on the eye than the blackness of Ramona's gaze.

"But–" she starts. "So we can reschedule - do this another time?"

I pause, allowing the gap between us to speak for me, wanting to get the message across without words.

She takes a step closer, leans in to connect.

"Sure," I say. "Another time."

I look up and she beams, the blemishes on her cheeks crinkling into grotesque scars.

"Good, because I'd like that," she smiles.

"Yeah?" I say.

She nods, and I see the fingers on her right hand spreading out, the knuckles more simian in the sunshine than the cloaking half-light of the coffee shop. Quietly, her hand begins to makes its way towards me, cutting through the air and seeking out my touch.

Bile rises once more, and I take a half-step back. I imagine that tiny hand balled up into a fist, ready to strike.

"Did you ever hit anyone?" I ask, the nausea confusing my senses.

"What?" She's taken aback, unable to cope with the change of pace.

"Hit me," I say, warming to the idea. "Hit me as hard as you can."

"What, no. I'm not doing that." She's confused, unable to disrupt her comfortable little world and try something outside of the ordinary.

The idea appeals more and more, of taking this baffled yeti and forcing violence from her. I want to feel the meagre force of her punch bouncing off my taut abs or chiselled jaw.

"Come on, hit me. Hard as you can," I say once more.

My words drift past her and to the people around us. No one stops, no one turns to see the show.

"Umm, why?" She takes a step back, the idea of connection less appealing now it's not on her terms.

"Why? I don't know – have you ever punched a guy?" I ask.

She looks confused, discomforted by this slice of reality. "No – I'm not that sort of person."

"Pah," I say.

"It's a good thing," she scowls.

"Come on – how much can you know about the world, about yourself, if you don't practice a little violence now and then," I say.

"God, this is crazy," she says, and begins looking around. To all sides, reality continues, unchecked, unmoved by our little fracturing of convention.

"Come on, no one's watching," I say. "Do it."

Her fingers have stopped flexing now, connection no longer sought.

"No, I don't think so," she says.

"Go on, the face, the gut – wherever you want. Surprise me," I say.

"This is so fucking weird," she says. "What's it all about – is it a joke?"

"A joke?" I ask.

"Yeah, I don't know. Sometimes I don't get jokes."

"No joke."

I hang my jaw out there, wait for the tiny fist to be hurled towards me, for the impact and the release.

The blow never comes. Girls, they just don't have it.

* * * *

"Where the fuck is Lolita?"

I hate it when the bitch moves my stuff around. Why can't it just stay where I leave it?

"What?"

"Lolita – my book. What have you done with it?"

"Nothing. Have you looked in your room?"

"It's not in my room. Otherwise, I wouldn't be looking down here, would I?"

Jesus, people can be slow.

"Here." Mum pulls a book from the side of the sofa and flings it across the room to me, bent pages fanning out as it flies through the air.

"This is Fight Club, Mum. I need Lolita. Lo-lee-ta."

She shrugs. I give up and move through to the kitchen. Doubt Mum would even recognise a book if she saw one, ignorant cow. Kicking a plastic bag swollen with rubbish across the floor, I search amongst the crumpled packets on the side. Most are empty, discarded. Lazy bitch never cleans up.

"Found it?" she calls from the living room.

I keep looking, opening cupboards, moving crap around as I go. It's got to be in the house somewhere – I've only had it two weeks.

I go back into the living room, pull the cushions off the end of the sofa that remains unoccupied. Nothing.

"It's only a book. It'll turn up, won't it?" Mum says, lighting a cigarette.

Humbert had the right idea – stick it to them while they're young and then get the hell out of there. They're not worth the hassle, women. Girls, though, they can satisfy the itch, but you've just got to beat them down before they have a chance to turn into the stubborn archetype.

"It's a library book – I've got to take it back, Mum."

She shrugs.

"Move."

I gesture for her to slide up the sofa.

"It's not here; I looked, didn't I?"

"Look again. I ain't got the money to pay for another lost book."

Fag hanging from her lips, Mum delves into the sofa with both hands.

"Nope."

"Fuck."

I stomp back upstairs and kick the door to my room open; it cracks off my wardrobe, the hinges creaking.

"Oi – pack it in!" Mum shouts from downstairs.

I shove the door closed and block the ignorant woman out.

Looking around, there's no sign of Lo. Not that there's too many hiding places. My single bed, covers thrown all over the place: signs of a good night. My desk, leaning unsteadily against my bed and covered with a few used bowls, the odd piece of discarded toast, and my laptop. A swing chair, the back broken clean off – this is where Lo should be, it's where my books live. My wardrobe, cheap and tiny, doesn't even hold my clothes, which spill out from the open doors and onto the grey-brown carpet, mixing with the normal cocktail of crumbs, dust, and condom wrappers. Shit. There's nowhere for Lo to hide. Even nymphets won't lower themselves to hang about in a place like this. Don't get me wrong, I've got everything I need. But fuck, life in a box isn't much to shout about. It's nothing but a holding pen for the inevitable, for the final box. State-sponsored housing? State-sponsored euthanasia.

I'll be alright though, I won't be one of these slobs who lives their whole lives in a place like this, medicating the days away. I've got plans. I'll take my lead from Dad – he was smart enough to do a runner, to claim his freedom from this shithole. Don't worry about me; I'll be out the door first chance I get. I'll have a room the size of a football pitch, and for every bedroom at least three bathrooms in my little mansion.

Shit, Lo's in the john – course she is. I was having a wank over her while I was on the bog yesterday: a neat little lumpkin.

I open my door and stick my head out. There's Lo, part-hidden beneath the u-bend. I go over to the bathroom and gather her up. She's not in bad shape all told – nothing the tight-ass librarians could complain about anyway. I wipe away a fleck of spunk – it's a good job they come ready covered in plastic. Wipe-down delights. I'll enjoy handing this one in round the old bibliotheque.

Looking down at tender Lo, I feel a twinge.

I close the lavvy door. One for the road.

* * * *

I'm a lone wolf, for the most part. It doesn't pay to have other people around. They slow you down, complicate things. No, you're better off alone, with a clear head and only your own impulses to be satisfied. That's the shit, that's the way to live.

These lads who go out drinking in huge gangs; I just don't see the point. They spend half the night shooting pool, pouring pints over each other, and 'bantering' like a bunch of fucktards. Where's the end-game? They're just wasting each other's time, distracting themselves from the main event. Maybe they've got the fear, maybe they're in it together, offering each other an excuse not to put themselves out there, to shoot for the pussy. Because that's what we're all out there for, right? All the lovelies tarted up in their skimpiest frocks are hardly going to be impressed by a horde of babbling apes who are struggling to keep up with the evolution they see all around them. No, they want someone with a little more subtlety, who's actually got the bollocks to drop the pretence, stalk right up to them and offer it up on a plate. Oh, they appreciate that. Who wouldn't?

These guys who hunt in packs, they haven't got a clue. Their only chance is for one of the tartier tarts to down one too many tequilas and drop their guard. They'll both enjoy the five minutes of sweaty groping back at her place then – in the moment at least; the next morning all memory will be wiped, the hangover descending. And this is how people live, how they breed. Nothing but denial and escapism from start to finish. The movie in their heads resembles the garbled glamour that Hollywood spews out, but the reality, well, they shield themselves from it at every opportunity.

Now, don't get me wrong, mates are alright, in their way. Back at college, I had the crew: Matty,

Jim, Smithy. The lads. We were all packing hard-ons 24/7 back then of course, couldn't turn our minds to anything but skirt, but you know what, those guys were sound. We'd shoot the shit in the park after college was out. Sipping on Dr. Peppers or something stronger if there was someone fresh serving in the offy. Yeah, that was pretty sweet. Watching the birds scuttle by in their groups, linking arms, and giving us all a thrill with their short skirts, and fuck-me halters. The craik was good in those days, we were on the level. Course, we never went out on the pull together – nah, none of the local establishments would have us back then. Oh, they'd slip the giggling girls in, but us boys, no, forget about it. They didn't need the competition.

You need a crew at college; guys to watch your back. Out here in the real world though, they're surplus to requirements. The boys, they all went off to uni – smart group we were, not all about the skirt, not quite. Course, none of them matched up to me in either department, but they were above the average, no doubt. We all knew it would end when we went off to uni though, pastures new and all that. Now and then we cross paths out there in the world, sloping round town or with some dame on our arms. There's the wink of recognition, but nothing more. We've all moved on. Ok, I chucked the system in; chose to remove myself from that little game. None of the lads really get it – they're out there being shaken down for thou after thou; their wallets, stomachs, and beds all pitifully empty. While I'm out here, milking the system, taking money out rather than throwing it away on a bit of paper, they're all scrabbling around with lardy tarts who haven't given a blowjob once in their lives.

No, I'm the winner of that little group, nice lads though they are. They're all too conformist for me. They don't think outside the box, outside reality. It's all down to their parents – those proud ma's and pa's who keep throwing money at their little darlings, hoping to maintain the illusion of comfort their kids are drowning in for as long as possible. Mugs. My lot know the score, not a penny for my education, and they were bang on it. Dad gets it, understands that it's all a con. You've gotta make your own life, outside of the rules. Nah, the 'rents weren't ever gonna stump up – they're too savvy to the world.

See, Dad's a lone ranger – like me. We're men of the world, we get it, understand how the game's played. We don't take no shit from the establishment, from anyone. Paying out all that dough for a slip of paper? No, no, no, that does nothing but make you the system's bitch, taking it squarely up the ass and paying out for the privilege.

And by the way, after all of those years of work and all the dollars dropped, what does an education actually get you? A pen-pushing job? Some squirrely existence in a secondary school somewhere, convincing the next generation that education is the thing – kidding yourself, kidding them. No thank you, friend, not for this fella.

I'm not saying school was a total waste of time – you

learn the ropes, enough to dispel the mist and see the world for what it is. The rest I can do myself, I don't need some fag in corduroy telling me that he knows the answers better than me. No, I live the life authentic: none of that intellectual, stick it up your Heidegger bollocks. Get real.

* * * *

The quiet thumping in my chest as blood rushes around my body, the stiffness in my muscles; it's the physical prelude to a session with Lexi. Not a fuck session necessarily, any session. It's that fire of adrenaline that puts you on top of your game, keeps you sharp.

Those moments between making visual contact and truly connecting – they're the shit – a voyeur to your own woman. Lexi looks stunning: a tight crop top holding up her weighty endowment and a flouncy skirt, short as fuck, which floats as she moves. Both baby pink – an outward innocence that convinces no one.

Mouth dry, I look on; watch as her body moves through the atomic air, disturbing everything around her from the molecular level up. She doesn't just inhabit space, she owns it. I stretch my muscles and pat my crotch to remind myself who's boss here, then engage:

"Hey, Lexi."

"Hey," she says, warmly, her inward heat bursting out and overwhelming me with its soft comfort. She's got this knack of making you feel like the centre of the universe, Lexi, like nothing's off limits to you, the top celebrity of her little world.

"How are you today, sweetie?" I ask. It's a wet entrée, I know. But it's all I need, just a semblance of conformity to grease the wheels, you know. Maintain the idea that you're one of the drones.

"I'm good, darling. Fantastic, in fact." She beams, more hot energy emanating from her slender frame.

"Yeah?"

You have to ask, it's not optional.

"Oh yes, I was playing with some *very* big boys earlier," she says.

She's a tease, Lexi. You can go with her or not, but she's one of these birds that equates everything to sex, responds by instinct, or perhaps by conditioning, to a sexual world.

"Cool."

"You know how I like my boys, don't you?"

She's got it on full beam tonight, sex sliding over her tongue before being spat back out into the world from where it first came.

"Yeah."

I don't need the details – you hold life together on the general thrust; once you get into details, everything comes apart.

"And how are you today, handsome?"

She leans in, her soft bosoms bulging towards me as she fixes me dead in the eye.

"Pretty good – been looking forward to talking to you."

"Oh yes?"

Her eyes relax comfortably as she pulls back, interested for the moment.

"Yeah, you know how you go through a day building up things to tell people - wanting to remember it all? Well, it's been a bit like that."

It's funny how that goes, how you write a narrative for yourself, edited for the benefit of a specific other.

"I see, and what sort of things have you been bursting to tell me?"

She pouts, her warm pink lips glistening.

"Oh, you know, nothing that interesting. Mum's being a pain in the arse today."

"Yeah?"

"Yeah, but she's always a bit like that, so you get used to it, I guess."

"Yeah."

She nods in recognition, acknowledging but nothing more.

"And there's this library book – it's late, I think. I'm going to get more fines – such a fucking rip-off. I'd much rather be spending the money on you; I'm glad you're here to take my mind off it all, anyway."

"Oh, well I can be *very* distracting."

That's another thing about Lexi, she talks in italics. It's a learned sensuality, a learned sense of expression that you find in all actors. And don't get it wrong, Lexi is a right little actress; she's a performance.

"Yeah, you can," I say.

"Maybe you need a little distraction right now?"

A turn of the cheek, a slightly raised eyebrow; it's

pantomime.

"Yeah, that would be good," I say.

"What would you like today then, Mr Big?"

Her eyes widen and she drops her head a fraction.

"Everything."

"Everything?" she purrs.

"Everything you've got," I confirm.

"You're a lucky boy, because I've got an awful lot."

She exhales and presses her body into beautiful contortions, designed to make a woman of her.

"I know."

"Let's go then, cowboy."

She's primed, ready to start the show, ready to compete in the feather soft arena.

"You don't want to chat a little bit first?" I ask.

"If you like; if you think you can wait for this," she says, as she brushes her hand over her soft curves.

"You're so hot."

"Thank you," she laughs.

"I want to fuck the shit out of you."

"Sounds good," she says.

"Real hard, like you like it."

"You know me so well, darling," she purrs.

"True."

"Let's go then, sweetie." Her lips part, and she exhales the words.

"Let's go."

* * * *

Will we ever go too far? Is it possible anymore? We don't have limits, don't do taboos. Death, that's the last taboo – that's what they tell you. Well fuck that, if that's your opinion, you want to plug in my friend, look up some of the shit people put out there. Death isn't personal anymore, isn't intimate – what is? You can look death straight in the face; it's only a few clicks away. Take this cunt, I just don't get it. Reading the last rights straight down a camera lens before he lets the claret flow, watches it seep out all over the place. What makes you want to do it? What's the point of being a celebrity after death? The nihilism is great, that's top – I get that. Even putting it out there, exposing the changeless reality of the world, fair do's, that's no bad thing. But come on, it's hardly the way to go. Who needs all that shit after they're gone – all the comments and bitching? Nah, there's enough of that in life.

Some of this shit is good viewing though, proper action stuff. Take a look here - and don't pull that squeamish shit, I know you want to see this as much as the rest of us - fix your eyes and don't be coy. You can see what's coming; train looming, fucking retard looking edgy. Whoof, look at that. Pow, splat. That's entertainment, my friend. You don't get that from Hollywood.

But if you like that sort of reality, try this out, this is the shit. I know what you're thinking: that broad's nothing special, good for her age, but just wait, see that wog with the baseball bat? You know where this is going, right? You don't need me to tell you where that barrel is headed. Oof, that's real shit, no?

And talking about video nasties, what about Saddam? Well, what about him? His little swansong hardly registers on the scale, does it? A lot of fuss about nothing. It's like when Paris Hilton shot that porno – who gives a fuck? There's plenty better tarts out there who do it twice as well. Just because you've seen her with clothes on, doesn't make it anything special. There's a million better videos floating about, Saddam is just a media celebrity like the rest of them: not worth the admission fee.

We don't need limits anymore, it's all out there, it's open. You want it, take it. Enjoy your own limits, my friend, but it's freedom – no one's stopping you, no one's condemning, not if they're the modern.

* * * *

Walking into a bookshop is a depressing thing. It's not the pretentious twats, browsing books as part of their desirable lifestyle. It's not the scrubby members of staff serving at the counter: the pseudo-hippies and fucking misfits. It's not the stink of coffee wafting out from somewhere in the building, a concession to the cult of the coffee bean. No, it's the books.

I could ignore the other shit, decide that maybe it didn't matter too much, that when consumerism meets culture, the result is always going to attract wankers and everything that goes with them. But the books, no, they're what make your stomach sink and that feeling of dark syrup on the brain descend.

Look around you, look at the shelves upon shelves of books – for years, the vessels of all knowledge. We're part of the new world now, but books persist. Cheap biographies, pulp fiction; glossy covers hiding inadequate sentiments. Walk in and you're surrounded by this shit – to every side a reminder that we don't want stimulation anymore, we want sedation. Fight your way through the celebrity memoirs, pornographic cook books, and cheap thrills that satisfy most and you get to the second wave of vomit-inducing product: offerings for the inspired and arty. Matte poetry books, classics, the finest culture can provide packaged and wedged into trendy coverings, kidding you that you're buying a fashion accessory, not a book.

But hey, if you can stomach a trip further into the shop, you hit on the meatier stuff – history, science, economics – provided they can stick 'pop.' in front of it, they'll stock it. Pop. psychology, pop. art, pop. life. It's the new world – we don't want serious anymore, we want nuggets of almost-useful information. Books are the past, they're on the out. Information is digital now; bookshops, they're somewhere between gallery and museum.

The girls in bookshops, though – they're easy prey. See, lads, they might be in a bookshop like this to pick up some real reading, or to play a part. Girls, they're oblivious to the shit that goes on, their heads are full of fluff and fantasies. In a place like this, they're all primed for action, ignorant to the cause. The girls on the checkouts too – they're open to a little conversation, a chance to open their minds.

Looking around, most people would be fooled into thinking there weren't any dames here, that these were straight cold cuts – nothing to offer the warm blooded. But, my friend, you've gotta look a bit closer. Most of these awkward sorts haven't been touched, haven't had their potential released. You've gotta look on them three fucks down the line, when they really blossom. This brunette here, the one with short frizzy hair and glasses; yeah, she's tipping the scales at a few pounds more than desirable, but you've gotta see the raw material. Slim her down a bit, slap a push-up bra on her, some product for the hair, and she'd be in pretty good shape, no? What about the gangly blonde over there? The one who's all elbows, and no curves? She's awkward to look at, I'll give you that, but you've gotta know that after you teach her how to fuck, she'll soon have that body of hers under control, will go from gangly to graceful in no time.

It's all in the potential, see? Most girls don't know what they have, don't know their true value. If you can unlock that in them, they're yours unconditionally. That's what you want – a world of broads all eternally grateful for your cock and what it's done for them. You don't need to be tied down to one – they won't demand the full works, only enough to reassure them that there's a future in this world. The girls that know what they've got, they're bullshit; they're for fucking and discarding. The needy ones, they're the daily pleasure; they're the stepping stone to the next evolution of the sexual life.

If you're picking out tail in a bookshop you've gotta know the score. Girls at the front, browsing bestsellers and biographies, they're only dipping their toes into the water, only feet from the exit, they're not committed, don't belong to this world. Those flicking through the cookbooks, they're the homely types – all commitment and not enough pussy to justify the investment. Girls on travel books are a possibility; dreamers, escape artists. You can offer them what they're looking for without needing a passport. They're rare though, and you've got to be careful because a lot are already involved, have someone else on the spin. Where you get the real fantasists, the one's with an engine to fulfil the other, well, that's the arty corner. The poets and painters, lyricists and guitar-strummers. Granted, there's not always a lot to choose from, but the hit rate is high enough that that doesn't matter. Drop a few semi-literate sentences and they're creaming before you've even asserted the physical.

Point in case, one tiny bird huddled up in the corner: head in some slim volume, she's oblivious to the creeping world in here, never mind the tangle out there. I browse shelves in her direction, the slightness of her frame growing ever clearer as I move closer. I peer over, try to catch a glimpse of the book that she's cupping in her petite paws. Nothing, some sort of poetry. No easy in then.

I look her over for inspiration – not much to go on from behind; pixie boots in firm leather – the best bet – plain black leggings and a non-descript jumper.

For people that are supposed to have the spark, arty types sure as fuck dress to be ignored. Her dark hair, cropped short, allows a look at her fragile shoulders – no necklace, a good sign. A necklace means ownership – a man, a past, a god. No, bare and untaken – that's a good sign.

I pull a book from a high shelf, impose my presence on the scene. Her head flicks slightly to the side, and wide eyes flit in my direction before jumping back to the book. She shuffles half a step towards the shelf in front of her and then another half step to her right, away from me. She's timid, afraid of life. I smirk.

Flipping open the book I've pulled off the shelf, I study it for a moment or two. The tiny sort to my right replaces the book she's been fingering with another. I look up, smile: "Looks interesting."

"I hope so," she says. With a half-smile flickering across her face, she opens the new volume and drops her eyes once more.

You can't appear too eager with this stuff; have to play it cool and let them come to you a little. I leaf through my own book a bit more, face the bookshelf and give her no attention. Looking more closely at the book I've unthinkingly pulled out, I notice it's some stupid lad-lit. A single guy who goes out drinking and looking for love – a feckless slob who somehow ends up with some tight piece of ass; senseless. I thrust it back onto the shelf in front of me and pull out another one. A William Burroughs, more carefully selected this time.

I examine the cover and then turn to check out how Little Miss is getting on. She's looking over inquisitively – this cat and mouse shit really works. I smile; it's on now, the ice has well and truly thawed.

She nods her head slightly towards the book I've just returned to the shelf. She doesn't seem the type, but maybe she's a fan. I pull the chunky lad-lit back out and offer it out to her, "Interested?"

She rolls her eyes and half-smiles again. Taking the book, she stretches up to the top shelf, her pointed boots creasing as she extends on to tip-toe to reach the too-high shelf. Dropping back to her natural height she straightens her jumper, "You should put them back where you take them from."

A little tension; no bad thing. I smile wider, "Yeah?"

She murmurs confirmation as she goes back to the book she's still clutching.

"Anything good?" I ask.

"John Donne," she says, flashing the cover at me. Some old prick stares out from a mock-plate in the centre of the artwork.

"Looks boring," I say.

"It's not," she says, and goes back to scanning the pages.

Slowly, she's turning the tables – it's something women do. Doesn't matter how long the timeframe is, they'll always end up on top, or so they like to think. But that shit doesn't work with guys in the know. Guys who understand you can't pander to their every need.

I turn my back on my elfin friend and scan the shelves

for a book that would make a good conversation piece. Something gently philosophical maybe, that'd do the trick. Women can't help but be flattered when you ask their opinion on something, can't wait to unfold their inner thoughts for you to soak up. Girls are trained to be philosophers – Cosmo asks them the small questions, prepares them for a life of searching and coming up short. Philosophy is just the natural extension; it's the big questions, the gratifying opportunity for self-absorption, the perfect excuse.

I pull *The Lightness of Being* off the shelf and flick through for a quick burst of inspiration. Finding a decent passage, I turn slowly, as though in mid-thought – you've got to be subtle here, disinterested – and, ready to drop a good, deep question, peel my eyes up from the page as though it's a real effort.

The cheeky bitch is three bookcases away, her boots having carried her silently across the carpet and out of my immediate range. Tricky, but not irretrievable. A situation like this calls for a little subtlety though. I push *Lightness* back onto the shelf and make my way ponderously over to where she now stands, moving by as though en route to the science section just beyond the literature. As I pull past her, I stop, pretend to notice something of interest on the shelf next to hers, and re-open, "Don't you hate the way they organise bookshops?"

She looks up, "I'm not sure. How do you mean?"

It's all part of the act, the feigned indifference, feigned ignorance – girls drop back to this act almost unconsciously.

"The way they put all the idiot books where anyone can find them, and hide all the proper books," I say.

She considers, "I suppose so," and goes back to her book.

Cold. Really cold. But that's ok, I've got more than enough to handle this. Time to pull out a jealousy sub-plot to our little story – that'll stoke the fires, no problem.

I edge away smoothly, not looking back at the impish stranger, and head for the checkout. There's a plump blonde girl with a scraggy string band around her neck, and beads on her wrist. Fucking hippies.

"Can I help?" she asks. Her face fixed, a smile catches on her lips, making it no further.

"Yeah, have you got a book called *Life is Elsewhere?*" I ask, leaning on the counter and locking eyes with her intently – it's human connection, it's the same old bullshit that we've bought into for years: eye contact equals emotional contact. It's bollocks, but enough people buy into it to make it worth using.

Her eyes break contact within a split second, as they flit down to her computer screen, her fingers flying across the keyboard as she enters my enquiry. "We don't have it in at the moment," she purrs, "but I can always order it for you?"

"It's ok," I say.

She's into the interaction now, it doesn't have to be anything special, it's all playing on the Donne groupie's inbuilt jealousy. I just need to keep the interaction going a minute more and then I can switch back to the primary target: "Can you see which other stores have a copy?"

"Oh, I don't know how to do that, I'm afraid. Hang on," she says, before calling around the corner, "Joel!"

I look over at the arty girl, now browsing a table display, Donne firmly replaced on his shelf.

A guy with matted hair and flecks of earthy stubble comes round the corner, "Can I help?"

The hippy girl wafts off and this lanky prick takes up the enquiry. This doesn't really work as a jealousy plotline.

"What are you looking for?" my new assistant asks.

It's a good question – a big question – but not one I'm giving him an answer to.

"It's alright," I say, and pull back from the counter.

"Oh, are you sure?" he says, looking slightly unsure, "I can look up stock across all our branches…" He trails off.

I stretch my lips out and up in what will pass as a smile, "It's fine."

"Ok then," he offers, "Have a good day."

"Yep." Smile gone, I turn and slide away, eyes averted. When I pull them back up, I search out the tiny terror. She's nowhere to be seen. Perhaps she isn't in on the game, perhaps she lost her bottle.

I look around for a new target. Nothing.

* * * *

The still air cracks and splinters under the strain. A weary tightness clasps my chest tight, and I focus on my breathing, soft breaths slipping from my slightly parted lips. Annabel looks on. I look beyond.

She runs the tip of her forefinger along the edge of her papers, caresses the scant notes she's kept on me. Insight no longer possible, it's the simple totting up of facts, the quantifying of the recordable. Am I unusual in my self-restraint? Probably. Most sad bastards can't wait to get in here and start blubbing their eyes out, weeping about what a lousy life they're having, and how none of it is really their fault. I wonder if she helps them scapegoat. That's what the headshrinkers are for, right? To tell you that you're ok, that your sad little life is all that could be expected when you consider what terrible traumas you've had to deal with: losing your ma for five minutes while at Brighton pier 20 years ago, abandoned to the will of strangers; how those kids at school called you names and asked you to justify your existence; how your boss just doesn't appreciate you, that you can see it in his eyes. Fuck. Whole books filled with this shit, page after page of meaningless bleating.

Does having all this moaning recorded make it feel more real, more justified? Does Annabel's interest give these sad fucks a sense of permanence, a solidity in this world? You'd have to have a pretty slim grip on reality for this hollow set up to add weight to your existence.

A quiet intake of breath threatens to break the silence. I relax, watch as Annabel pulls her hand away from the notes, a small nick on her forefinger. A paper cut from her persistent note stroking. Barely a drop of blood; it's all she'll give.

"Don't you just hate paper cuts?" she says, standing up and reaching for a tissue on her desk.

I sigh, fix my gaze on the wall. What's the point of small talk? This is a place for big talk, and once you've decided against that then it's just a case of counting out the minutes.

"How's the medication going?"

I let my eyes pull slowly over to Annabel, heavy lids dipping as I do so.

"Fine."

There's not much you can say really. They need to know that you're not abusing the meds, that you aren't putting them to uses beyond the obvious. Course, that's the whole point of accepting them, isn't it? Fine little stockpile I've got now – always something on for a big night out. Uppers, downers; you name it, I carry it. All officially signed off and paid for by the government. The state are the biggest pushers of all – they want to keep you happy and compliant, and what better way than the tiny powder pills? Delicious.

Annabel, she hasn't got a clue. Course, she buys into the whole drugs as a 'clinical tool' line, doesn't see the big con, the grand scheme. But why would she, she's vacant to the world? So I'll happily hoover up all they throw at me – store them up and put them to good use on a night out.

"So, you'd say there's been a change in your mood?" she asks.

Since when? It changes all the time, you dopey cow. Right now it's bored, verging on lethal. Tonight it will be pumped. Tomorrow, deflated after some heavy action. How's your mood, you stupid bitch?

"How's Mum?"

There's a comfort in the familiarity of the questions – she's not all that creative, Annabel Bird. Straight from the textbook: A, B, C. Good job humans are so predictable, good job the masses follow a pattern, don't fall outside the template.

"How's Dad?"

If walking out was an option, I'd be gone. I'd check in, sign my name, and walk back out into the world where people don't hide their indifference. Can't do it though. If I did, Annabel would be straight onto the social to tell them I'd been skipping out. More hassle than it's worth. So it's head down, and trudge through this shit. You don't mind jumping through a few hoops when you see the end goal, when you realise how absurd the whole thing is. It's the poor fuckers that don't see the truth, they're the ones you gotta feel sorry for: shunted around the system without any choice in the matter. Brain-dead fucking lemmings.

The scratching of Annabel's pen irritates my senses as it records the void. I fix my sight on the cheap, whitewashed wall, willing my gaze to penetrate the heavy bricks and escape the oppressive office. I can feel my teeth clenching together, slowly grinding under the strain.

Annabel looks up. I look beyond.

* * * *

Depression, they say. Maybe. Borderline. Have they taken a look at me lately? Bang on it sweet cheeks, fucking lovin' it out there. I dip my wick nightly and fucking stalk the streets and the snatch every day. Can they be serious? But of course they can. I've seen the reports, it's all tied up with the social – they're in it together, holding back the benefits if I don't make my weekly appearance in the interrogation room. They're just looking for an excuse not to pay out. You don't want to know about that though, about all the bullshit they're trying to drop on me. I'm sound as a pound, and cocked for war.

* * * *

The midday sun exposes the harsh reality of life as we know it; there's no hiding place in its illuminating glare. All down the high street, people bustle and hurry, no one noticing the fresh clarity the light throws on their surroundings. Some rest their hands on their foreheads, trying to block out the light, to hide from its penetrating rays. Others slip into the shadows, allowing their eyes to be enclosed by the more familiar gloom, and keeping themselves out of the limelight. The heat is enough to put some people off entirely, others hide their tender heads under hats, or block out the world with sunglasses. No one is willing to accept this reality; everyone feels the need to shy away from it, to create their own version of it.

Around me, streams of people drive forward, perfect processions from one hiding place to another. Movement is everywhere, but I'm still, my eyes refusing to blink away the blistering light. Sitting on a wall, the rough edge of the brickwork presses through my jeans and into my flesh, ready to punish anything but stillness on my part with a graze, a small nick.

I am one moveless pole of this swarming reality. Opposite me sits the other: a grubby pavement-dweller. A street-whore. I glare straight over at her, but she doesn't look up, her face firmly pointing downwards, examining a scrap of newspaper that sits in her lap. You can almost smell the matted tangle of her hair from over here, twenty feet away. Dirty bitch.

With her head bent, the people that pass by feel free to take a good look at what society does to those it considers surplus to requirements. Their glances – derisory, sympathetic – are all for show anyway. This filthy layabout doesn't evoke any real emotion, doesn't provide anything more than a sideshow. And why should she? She's made her choices, taken herself out of the flow of life. She can't expect sympathy, not really. She's lucky to have accumulated the meagre collection of shrapnel that covers the fraying rug in front of her. It's more than she deserves.

Even the people that part with their loose change don't really empathise – they do it to make themselves feel better, to assure themselves and everyone else that they are a good person, that they deserve the fortunate hand fate has dealt them. Fucking deluded. If people dropped all this pretence and just got on with the life authentic, they'd leave scabby skanks like this one to rot. Leave them to fall out of an existence in which they have no purpose.

There's nothing to tell you this one's any different, has any hidden value to this world: she wears the same wretched shades of grubby despair, the same filthy layers that they all do. All these street people, they design themselves to blend in, to fade out of the collective consciousness. Shit. Stick on a bit of colour, you sad pricks: where's this get-up getting you?

Still, they're not far off the rest of society, are they? Everyone designed to blend in, to belong to a group that hides their individual frailties, protects them from being exposed out here, alone and vulnerable. It's a fucking joke. The individualist West, where everyone hides and no one wants the spotlight. Those few that do, most of them are backwards, dreaming up a dream that doesn't exist in this world. It's down to the tiny handful – the ones who really understand this place – to take it on, to emerge from the crowd and move humanity forward a few steps.

Some lads walk past the skank, one grabs his crotch and thrusts it in her direction. They laugh, slap each other on the back. One sniffs his fingers, another flicks out his tongue. They barely break stride, all throwing friendly punches at each other and looking back to the street-slut. She remains unmoved, her face still pointing straight down. There are a few tuts from the passing crowd – moments ago aimed at the victim, now directed at her abusers. No one stops. Mild emotions are always transferable; their target isn't important, they exist solely for the benefit of their originator.

From beyond the wretched whore, I catch a glimpse of a familiar face: Matty. He's swinging his way through the crowd, some dolly bird on his arm. His new squeeze, I guess. The one from uni: it didn't take Matty long, not even a term to get into her knickers. As they get closer I take a good look – she's nothing special. Dolled up with too much make-up and no real body on her. Matty pulls her close though, their arms linked and their hips bumping gently every few steps. Close enough now, I stand, call out, "Matty," but he's too busy whispering into his new slut's ear. I cut across the shoppers, catching the odd flailing bag.

"Oi, Matty."

He turns, pulling his girl to a stop. I close the gap between us.

"Hey," he offers, "I didn't see you there."

His clothes are crumpled, and he has the look of someone no longer cared for, but he's still somehow more together, more complete than he ever used to be.

"What's up?" I ask.

I see his girl's eyes running me over, appraising the cock-slinger she sees before her. I don't mind, they've got to get their fill somehow.

"Nothing much," he says. "Just shopping."

"Cool." Looking at this chick up close she's not so bad; nice eyes. Better than anything Matty scored before.

"Yeah," he says. His girl's eyes are wandering already. Surveying the rest of the high street, she puts gentle pressure on Matty's arm. Lardy cunt. As though she can't stop for two minutes.

"Back from uni?" I ask.

"Yeah, summer, innit?"

I shrug, "Nice."

"What you doing at the moment?" he asks.

"Just chilling out, you know? Do you still see the lads?"

"Sometimes. Not that much." He looks away, his gaze following his girl's.

"Cool," I say, thrusting my hands into my pockets.

"Yeah," he says. "We're supposed to be meeting someone," he nods at his girl.

"Cool," I say. "We should all meet up sometime."

"Yeah," he says. "That would be cool."

"Nice."

We slap palms like we used to; an affectation back then, barely that now.

Matty and his squeeze head on up the road and I go back to the wall. The grubby skank's eyes follow me, the newspaper in her lap no longer holding her interest. I stare back, and as I settle myself again, her lips contort into a half-smile and she goes back to her newspaper.

* * * *

"Hello, trouble." I smile as I see Chloe; her face pale, her eyes made up with deep, dark eyeliner.

She smiles back, "Hello."

In her loose hoodie and tight vest top she's got a kind of grungy charm, I'll give her that. Ok, I like the pretty girls – the ones who fit the ideal, but Chloe, well, you've got to give it to her: there's something dark – risky almost – about her at times.

"How's it going?" I ask, wondering if she's bothered to wear a bra today – it hardly seems worth it for those bee-stings.

"Really good; I've been working on this." She reaches into her bag and pulls out a sheet of paper, barely bigger than her hand, and holds it out to me. I look closely, struggling to pick out the tiny details in the scratchy ink sketch. The fractured black lines run into one another, picking out a ghostly shape: a girl – Chloe, I guess – surrounded by shapeless apparitions who claw at her.

"That's fucking weird."

"Don't you like it?"

Fucking hell, what's to like? A bunch of scrawl on a scrap of paper – it's not exactly art, is it? Picasso wouldn't have got away with that shit.

"No, it's cool, I guess. What's it mean?"

I look more closely, trying to see the inky girl's face, trying to read her expression: nothing. There are shades that imply features, but they don't amount to anything. I frown.

Chloe stuffs the picture back into her bag, "It's nothing anyway; just something I was doing on the tram."

Odd little fucker, Chloe. I move closer, wonder

whether it's too early to turn things up a notch – whether the conversational part of the interaction has been fulfilled. She raises her eyebrows slightly. I smile.

* * * *

The uncomfortable time between day and night. Everyone's on edge, rushing away from the past or towards the future. No one's static, content with their current place. Nervous energy is everywhere – on a big night, when the atmosphere is ripe, it'll infect you, get into your bones. Most night's though, it's anxiety. The unsettled and ever-moving reality we live in. People, they shut themselves away from it, avoid the rush at all costs. You can't blame them – most people, they belong to the day or the night. No one wants to stray into the no man's land between the two – gives them the fear, gives them a taste of the foreign. No, they want to be cocooned up in their safe little worlds, away from the shifting reality of the real world.

It's a dangerous time to be out without a purpose. If you're not caught in the tangle of the transport network, you don't have too many options: the boozer, while the day-time drunks make way for the bright bingers, or the hypermarket, open 24/7, a scorching beacon of glass and concrete in the urban jungle. That's about it.

You don't want any part of the boozers at this time of day – they're full of podgy accountants and plastic secretaries. The dull, the snobby, the fucking dregs. Get down there for a pint during the day if you wanna hear some real wisdom, meet some real men of the world.

Or save it until night has properly descended, when the alcohol has taken effect, and everyone's out for a good time.

The supermarket, well, that's an untapped resource. It's not glamorous, but it's got all the essentials: the college chicks on the tills, working their evening jobs; the lonely office hags who pile their trolleys high with dinners-for-one, reeking of desperation; some decent eye-candy amongst the young mums too, bulging with their newly-ballooned figures as they deflate back to the norm.

It's a ripe market, if you know what you're doing. And the beauty of it all? Well, there's no competition. There's the sad blokes hurtling towards middle-age, their bodies buckling under the pressure of the journey. They'll all be packing a hard-on through their stained corduroys at the till, wheezing stale breath over the bored dolly-birds who bleep through the items without making eye contact more than twice. They're no competition, they're barely in the game, quietly slipping out of contention.

Then there's cheeky dads who still fancy having their ego massaged by exchanging a few hot words with one of the cashier lovelies. They're welcome to it – they haven't got anything else to offer, no end-game. Occasionally, if you make the mistake of shopping at the weekend, you get all these oily little shits, stocking up on budget vodka. They're always game for a crack at the dolly birds in their sexless uniforms. Every now and then one of the girls will buy into their chat, agree to a party or giggle at their shitty lines. But you'd have to be daft in the head to turn up at the weekend, knowing the risk of running into these little wankers. Tuesday, that's the day for the supermarket.

Hitting the edge of the estate, you can see the shoppers scurrying around inside, beeping things in and out of their baskets, each with their own agenda.

I'm primed for it tonight. Eight days since the last benefit cheque hit Mum's account so the shopping list is short – just the essentials, the cheap belly-fillers – this is perfect; you want to be travelling light when you're in the game. Tonight, well, it feels like a good night for chasing skirt. I'm fresh, haven't been sucked dry for a couple of days so I'm sharp but not on edge, looking good and feeling ready for a real chase.

Last week, there was this pretty dame on the checkout. A real Barbie girl – blonde extensions, a fat dollop of make-up, and a gold chain tracing the path to her cleavage from between the open collar of her shirt – she was up for it, no mistake. While I was doing the whole hunter gatherer bit, she rolled her metal cage around, never far from me, and always paying attention. You've gotta be cool in a situation like that, you don't wanna rush in like some eager twat, no. So I played it cool, gave her the eyes whenever I turned down a new aisle and found her there waiting for me. She was mad for it, no question. And you know what? When I came to pay, who was there on the tills, twiddling her hair and playing it innocent? Sneaky tart. I could have bent her over the desk and fucked a good inch of make-up clean off her face. I played it cool though; you can't just rush into these things. When she gave me the receipt I turned to my trolley for just a second, cold like, showing her my back. That gave me a moment's privacy, see. I scrawled my number on the receipt and flicked it onto the desk for her as I headed out. That's cool, my friend.

So now I'm following up on that, and seeing if there's an upgrade available – there's always an upgrade available. If you can play the dames off against each other you can really earn yourself a treat.

The juddering metallic sound of trolleys being driven across coarse tarmac irritates my thoughts as I approach the citadel. Pausing outside, I look into the painfully bright shop and check out the birds on the tills: Barbie isn't there, not that I can see anyway. Some lard-arsed cunt is in the way though. Smoking her fag and standing just where I need to be to see the last two checkouts. I get a little closer, marvelling at the gargantuan rump on my obstacle. She turns her head, her face plump and vaguely familiar, but I look past her and see that the final two checkouts are unoccupied. Shit. Maybe Barbie's stacking shelves again.

Lard-arse turns her body, giving the shoppers a full view of her prize asset, and I see the bloke she's smoking with. Baggy jeans and a white t-shirt, his skin tanned and creased, his face the same, gruff, with tight curls: a dirty blonde.

"What you looking at, son?" he smirks.

"Alright, Dad."

He nods at the woman, "Casey."

"Alright," I nod.

She acknowledges me but goes on sucking on her cigarette, blowing smoke and groaning gently.

"Bum us a smoke, Dad?" I say.

"Fuck off, tyke. Here's all I got. Bad for you anyway, innit?"

He flashes a packet at me, but I don't look down.

"Your Mum sent you down the shops then, has she? Lazy cow. Still at home bleating on about her back, is she?"

He grabs his back and staggers around, fag hanging from lips, ash sprinkling his t-shirt as he mimes.

Casey snorts. I grin.

"Yeah, slumped in front of the box like a fucking slug," I say.

Dad grabs me round the neck with his arm – I feel the wiry strength as he draws me close, half-headlock, half-hug. "She don't change, does she? Mardy cow," he says, scrubbing my hair like when I was a kid.

"Get off, you wanker," I laugh.

"Wanker is it?" he says, pulling me closer. I can feel the blood running into my face, "Cheeky sod."

I struggle but he keeps hold – strong guy, Dad.

Casey whacks him on his free arm, and tilts her head.

"Alright, alright, darling," Dad says to Casey. Letting me go, "Tell your Mum 'Fuck you' from me," he grunts and grabs up the shopping bags, which lie discarded around him.

I fix my hair and watch Dad amble off towards his

van, his wide, easy gait the sign of another swinging dick. He knows the score, Dad. Halfway up the car park he aims a heavy bag at Casey's monumental arse. He's a balls out player.

* * * *

If anyone tells you we don't have to live this way, then call them out. Jump right on that shit. We're not redeemable. Not even close. Anyone that says different is kidding themselves: we are that bad, there is no way back. If you only took half a moment to look, look back to the start. There is no game to lose any more: these are the new days, the infinite days. It's me and you, you and me. Opposition is gone, there's no need to take sides any more. We passed up our chance, embraced the future. We are it, we are forever.

* * * *

The moment you wake up, you can tell what sort of bird you've been with the night before – you don't need a blow by blow – it's all there, in your body; the map to your existence. A good night with Lexi and you wake up with your cock hard and red raw from too much action. That's a feeling my friend, that's the one.

You can forget about that after a night with the tiny Kraut. Fucking earache and a stiff neck from seeking the quiet life, nodding along, giving in to the tide. Some of us don't need the hassle, love; some of us haven't got time for the cause.

Try telling that to one of these lot though: they don't

get it, don't understand how you can reach different conclusions than they do from the jumble out there. How you can look at the tangle that is this world and conclude that we're anything but doomed. But let me tell you, some of us understand a bit more than you think, my friend. Some of us know this place intimately.

See Chloe, she's alright, but she doesn't know when to give it a rest. Sometimes you just want to talk shit and enjoy the flow. After being left hanging for hours, I had all this energy that I needed to release, see. If it was down to me, we'd have done the physical: got down to some serious grinding to the music. Hell, I like watching a broad shaking her hips as much as the next guy, even if she's barely got hips to shake.

But Chloe, she had other ideas. Didn't see where a little closeness could have led. Ok, she might not be sharp on this stuff like me, but fuck, a bulging crotch is hardly a subtle hint. Not when you're packing heat like I am.

Still, it's maybe for the best. Ok, she probably wouldn't be able to handle me in the sack anyway but, honestly, who needs the hassle? Once you give them the full show, they never leave you alone. It's an animal thing; once you spend a night making them cum, they get all attached. It's bollocks. Shouldn't we have evolved out of that shit years ago? Even in Darwin's day, the fellas knew the score, didn't hang around unless they got trapped with the old nine-month time bomb. Woman's last defence.

See, that's the worry when you get into anything

with a bird: the clingy-ness, the commitment. Keep it simple: shag the ones that give you that twinge, and keep well out of the rest. Soon as you give them an inch, they just want more and more.

Sometimes Chloe's not too bad. We sit down and just talk about how fucked the world is – that's the stuff, she gets that shit. Ok, if you let her, she'll start breaking balls about how it's our responsibility to change things – fuck that – but if you keep her on track, don't let her wander, then you get to the heart of it all. The black, putrid heart of this place.

* * * *

Bombs made of flesh and bone explode as they meet the pavement, a dull crack and splatter the only indication that the shower of colour in front of you is a life changing form, leaving its bodily home and returning to the atomic air.

9/11 is the only truly modern massacre to date. As the towers fell, cameras, some wielded by passers-by, others by news crews who fled to the scene, recorded everything, moment by moment. But what did they show on television? The steaming towers, collapsing over and giving way? Slack-jawed Americans weeping into their big Macs as their horizons were altered?

Shit – talk about manufactured reality. Where was the real stuff? The bodies broken beyond recognition, the screams of the dying? Sure we got the sickly sweet phone calls from those whose destinies had crept up on them. The messages of love, of regret. But hate, violence;

it was segregated, shown only in wide-shot under the sober commentary of some plastic newscaster. If you want reality you have to seek it out. It's all out there; plug yourself in and enjoy.

Here, try this – a compilation of the greatest hits of the Tuesday morning that captivated the world. Watch as edgy fuckers hang to windowsills, terrified to live, terrified to die. It's the perfect metaphor, the perfect image. But woof – look at them go, hurtling towards their perfect moment. Ten seconds – that's what they say – from release to impact; ten seconds of liberation as they cut through quickly thinning air. And then there is only mist.

Thousands of photos and videos record the fact. Log in, open your mind a little. Photos are all lies. They capture only a moment – a fall frozen. Worse still are the sidewalk images, stills that show a mess of debris, nothing to identify humanity from garbage. Fuck it, photos are of no value here. Video, that's what you want, my friend. The body in transit, the sound of extermination, of hope extinguished. It's video all the way – everything else is just fake or bullshit.

* * * *

"You know... you're pretty sweet really."

What a fucking mug, what a lightweight. Why doesn't she open her eyes – I'm no asshole, but 'sweet'? Give me a break, love. It's always this way with the soppy, sappy, doe-eyed ones. I didn't pick Chloe out for that at first, didn't see her as a traditional. Nah, she was new school when we first hooked up: fresh, angry, disconnected. What the fuck happened?

"I know you like to put on a front... but underneath, you're a nice guy."

Jesus fuck. What can you say to this sort of thing? How do you break it to them, explain that it's not a front, that it's reality through and through? You can't be a 'nice guy' anymore; they don't finish last these days – they're not even at the races. If you've dragged yourself this far in this world, in this life, then my friend, you are not a 'nice guy'.

"You should let it out more... I love it when you open up a bit."

The con, the great lie. They all want you to open up. At least, that's what they tell you – they demand a bleeding heart and then trample all over it when it doesn't suit, when they don't like what's on display. I expect better from Chloe, less of this shit and more of the other.

"Hey, are you ok over there?" she says, shuffling closer.

"Yeah."

"What are you thinking?"

It's the sympathetic bollocks now, the wide-eyed, gentle enquiry.

"Stuff... nothing that you want to hear."

"I always want to hear – you can tell me anything."

* * * *

Have you ever tasted a virgin cunt? It's the sweetest thing – prickling with sweat and damp with anticipation. Bury your face deep into that my friend, drink it in, inhale the pleasure. Christ, doesn't it make you hard just thinking about? Imagining spreading those lips and driving your heavy cock deep into that tight pussy. Hear the slag moaning as you split her wide open. Fuck, that's reality.

* * * *

Carnations or roses? As long as they're pink, Lexi will like them, guaranteed. She's a bird, isn't she? I'm not good at all this shit, but it's the thought that counts, right? That's what the soppy twats tell you. Could be a load of bollocks, but a bunch of flowers offers pretty good returns if you ask me.

I suppose it's all conforming to the fantasy, making her the Disney princess she's dreamed of being since she was four years old. Powerful stuff, playing along with the fantasy every now and then, getting deep into a bird's subconscious and unlocking something in there. Girls love it, lap it up, breathe heavy on that shit.

And look, Lexi's out of town at the moment, so there's no instant reward on this. But that's not the point; they keep it all bottled up, see, let it grow inside them. Then, when you do see them, well, that's a spectacle, my friend. It all goes off then.

I don't mind playing Prince Charming on occasion anyway – I've got it in me, I'm rough and sweet, sweet and rough. If you stick around, you'll see that.

So a mixed bunch it is. She'll love these, they're just the thing. And this is a bonus, a real movie moment for Lex. With the time difference, it's difficult to catch up at the moment, but we hooked up a few nights ago. Just a quick chat to let me know how she's making out (loving it), and when she's likely to be back (couple of weeks). Anyway, normally, when it's been a while, all I want to do is get down to a little show and tell, but I was wiped, so we kinda just chatted for a bit. I know, hardly a nut-buster, is it? But then she mentioned a job she had coming up in the next few days – a precious piece of information. So these pink buds will be waiting for her when she arrives at the gig in Miami. She won't see it coming, probably doesn't reckon I've got it in me. A small investment for a big pay-off, my friend.

Plus it lets her know who really cares for her, makes sure she doesn't get too caught up on the sweet meat of Yankland and forget where her bread's truly buttered. Yes indeed, when she steps off that aeroplane in a couple of weeks' time, she'll be creaming for a taste.

* * * *

The receptionist, a grotesque gargoyle with the stony personality to match, glares at her monitor, ignorant to the world around her. A scrawny girl with a terrible haircut comes scuttling through the door, and immediately the receptionist's face comes to life, all maternal concern.

"Hello, dear, what can I do for you?"

The girl mumbles and the gargoyle taps something

into her computer, her expression caught between her two worlds. She indicates for the girl to sit down with a reassuring nod and a half-smile. The girl does, and the gargoyle's features seize up once more. Pressing her glasses up her bulbous nose, her eyes fix on the computer screen; an unseen land, which only she is privy to. Us scum out in the waiting room are blind to her world, blinkered indefinitely.

I roll my tongue around my mouth, breathe in the warm, dusty air. The skinny girl sits two seats away, clothes hanging from her body, her body hanging from her soul. Drugs. Definitely drugs.

Annabel Bird appears from round the corner, where the offices hide. She looks at me and smiles from the mouth.

"Ok?"

She turns and heads back to the office. I follow. It's a wordless routine, the comfort of familiarity mixed with the anxiety of the event. Annabel's brown crumpled skirt sways as she walks, disturbed but barely moved.

As we turn into her room she offers me the usual chair and sits down opposite. The set-up would be confrontational if either of us gave half a fuck about what happens here.

"So, how've you been this week?"

Psychology-101. I sigh, my hands already in the pockets of my comfiest hoodie.

"Fine."

She pauses, looks at me. It's the same old tactic, the discomfort of silence. I let my head rock back and let out a low groan.

"That doesn't sound fine."

I roll my head forward and look at her, expressionless.

She moves her pen from one side of her clipboard to the other. Stasis all but maintained.

"How's Mum?"

I hold my breath, stop everything.

She doesn't notice, just sits there.

I close my eyes, let my chin drop into my chest. My ears pound and the world becomes indistinct.

"What are we doing?" she says from the blackness.

I hear Annabel move from her chair, feel her place a tentative hand on my shoulder. I let my body go limp at the waist, roll forward. Annabel drops to her knees, following my movement. Pressing her small hands against my shoulders she tries to heave me back in the chair but I let my dead weight fall against her meagre force.

"Are you ok?" she asks, firmly, cutting through the haze.

I open my eyes. Blink. Annabel's plain, taut face hovers inches from my own.

I scream, loud and long.

* * * *

Easing back, I relax into the soft, comfortable chair. The plush covering soothes my burning skin, hot with activity, and I let my heavy lids fall shut; a chance to refresh, to take stock.

My breathing slows, but the thump of my heart

continues to beat insistently against my ribcage. I rest one hand on my chest and soothe the overactive muscle. Things begin to calm, my senses untangle themselves as, with my eyes closed, the darkness comforts me.

The tiny hairs on my legs tingle, and my bare feet graze the deep carpet as I run them gently back and forth. Surrounded by softness, I feel weightless, every inch of my body supported, caressed. Breath seeps from my lips as I let go a low, contented groan.

Silky softness tickles my shins and I feel a single finger running up my calf, disturbing the matted order of the hair it passes over. As it reaches my knee, I feel two hands reach up and grasp my thighs, weight once more restored to my body as the unseen woman uses my frame to pull herself in against me. The soft movement of her hair tickles my thighs as her mouth seeks out its target. Blood rushes, and she doesn't hesitate long in going about her purpose. As the wet caresses send the familiar electricity around my body, I lean back, eyes still closed, and reach down to run my hand through this angel's hair.

Following her movement, directing it in its shadow, I listen for the familiar, muffled gulps that reassure me I'm more than a mouthful. The tender flesh of her cavity provides a comfortable pocket, and I feel my body tauten once more, the heat of activity spreading through me.

Opening my eyes, I look down at the mass of fierce red hair spreading across my thighs, its owner faceless but diligent. I look past the pale back that extends out from my waist and onto the carpet, and see only a blur of colours: peaches, blues, yellows. I blink, a sea of flesh snaps into focus. Girls, men, women: bodies tangle violently, ageing flesh rubbing up against smooth nubile skin. Rolls of fat smother muscled bodies, hard and soft meeting in vicious combat. A general murmur of satisfaction drifts through the air as the mass confirms that all is well, punctured occasionally by the sounds of violence that precede nirvana. From across the room, it's impossible to connect, everyone's eyes sagging to halfway shut, energy focused not on the bodies around them but internally, to their own self.

Amongst the shapelessness of the whole, stray body parts are visible, losing sensuality and gaining instead the eroticism of a powerful structure, a man-made ode to the gods. This collective, they're not sex, they're power, freedom. I look down at the head bobbing between my legs and, grasping it with both hands, pull it in close, choking the faceless vessel, as I slide into her throat and release my own burden into her.

* * * *

"Do you ever wonder if it's all worth it?"

She does bleat on about some daft shit, Chloe.

"What?" I say. It's a stall and we both know it – the conversation is coming, deflection is barely a possibility, and the Kraut looks like she's getting into her stride here.

"Well, life, I suppose. All of it," she says.

What else is there, after all? It's the big question, the

146

unknowable. And yet every amateur philosopher wants to take a stab, wants to puzzle it out. It always ends the same way, of course – the way it begins – in ignorance.

"Not really."

There's always a chance of blunting the conversation, bringing it to a premature end. But most people, see, they don't really need two people for a conversation; they're happy enough to have white noise fill the gaps, to account for their pauses for breath.

"You don't?" she says. "Because I was thinking, and I think maybe there is some point to it all, but you have to decide what the point is for you individually. I think it's love, don't you? That's what we all live for."

Love? She's having a laugh, isn't she? Love – no one lives for it, love's just our tranquiliser of choice, the thing that disguises this reality we're all existing in. And since when did Chloe get into all that fucking nonsense? She's straight, but she's always had that nihilistic streak.

"Nah, everything's meaningless isn't it? We're all just rotting flesh waiting to be put in the ground really."

"I don't think so," she says.

"No?"

"Stop it."

And we're there – that wasn't so painful after all. A quick change of pace, and we're putting all this shit to one side.

"Ok," I agree.

She pauses and bites her lip. The silence builds between us, an invisible wall that divides the already divided. I breathe heavily, let my chest collapse into a sigh. She looks down and continues nibbling on her slim lip.

"What do you want to talk about then?" I ask. My tone lets slip the slight exasperation creeping into my body.

She shrugs her shoulders. Perhaps we're not done after all, perhaps she's just regrouping, preparing to come back from another angle. When a lip-flapper's got something to say they rarely let the listener's complete disinterest sway them. After all, they just want to let it out, to 'express' themselves.

"Hey, I saw your president person on the news yesterday," I say.

"Chancellor."

"Oh yeah, chancellor – the dumpy bird."

She smiles. Puffing her chest and rounding her arms, she blows out her cheeks, and rolls her eyes in a grotesque impression of Frau Deutschmark.

I smile back as she holds the pose and then breaks into laughter. I join in, the comfortable noise fighting out the silence and purifying the stagnant air that hangs between us.

"She's an idiot," Chloe adds, when she's finished laughing.

"She's a politician."

We're on safe ground here: a common enemy, easy territory. This is what you want; the easy targets, the roundly despised.

"Yeah, bloated capitalists – they're the same

everywhere, yes?" Chloe offers.

"They're the same here."

"Why do people vote for them?" she wonders.

"I don't know. At least it's not like America, where they let bible-bashing retards run the country."

"It's true. It's always worse somewhere else."

She's got a point, but the Yanks have got it right in some ways. They know how to treat the weak, how to filter society so the cream rises to the top – all with a smile on their faces and God in their hearts. It's quite a dream they're operating over there, quite a reality they've constructed and sent around the world. Course, I'm not about to let on – me and Chloe, we're in this together right now. The Yanks are the common enemy, and they deserve to get both barrels – they can take it.

"America's a stupid fucking country anyway – what makes them think they should be running the world when they're full of fat, stupid morons? They think they're the future, but they're just a shallow, washed up sham of a country," I say.

"I want to go some day," Chloe says.

"Me too."

* * * *

You've gotta put it up these lardy tarts. Fuck with the tight-lipped cunts. So that's the game, that's what I do to pass the time. If you want to have a bit of fun then you've got to freak them out, my friend; give them that shudder, inside. My favourite is to stare them out – turn their game on its head. But here's the thing, and this is where a lot of people go wrong, I reckon. They stare the headshrinkers out by looking them in the eye. Oh no, that's the mistake: they're ready for that, see – they soften, try to draw you in, see that something in you. Fuckers. No, you've got to pick a point behind them – a crack on the wall, anything – and stare that bastard down. Look right on at that crack and don't move, not a muscle. If you can manage it, don't blink either. That's the shit. And when they talk to you, they throw out questions, start noting things in their little fucking books – well, you just keep on staring. Careful though, I've done it for whole sessions sometimes – that's the shit – but let me tell you, your eyes get pretty fucking sore if you're not blinking. Sometimes they water up a bit, so you gotta be careful – you don't want them thinking that shit means something. I've got caught out like that before. Staring down the wall while they ask you the same fucking questions, and then you start to blur up and they think they're getting through. And by then it's too late, you have to blink and those hot 'tears' are gonna drop down your face. Oh, they're all empathy then. Unless they're scribbling in their books.

But you know what? Fuck it. All the better if they think they're getting through to you. Keep them on their toes, maintain the illusion.

Imagine if they actually got a full burst of reality, if they really understood what people like us are all about – they'd shit their pants, call it a day. We don't need their sort. These headshrinkers are here for the weak, the ones that'll be picked off before long. They must see it, that they're only delaying the inevitable. That all these weeping pussies who come crying to them about what Daddy didn't do for them, or about how they're so fucking lonely because their cat just fell under a bus, well, they're on the way out. They're the old school, the outsiders.

And see, that's why there's no point me being here: I'm the new school, I'm beyond this stuff, the rules have changed but only the select few have been notified. Annabel Bird, she belongs to the past, this is the future.

* * * *

You heard about Tracy-May? Only up the duff – dozy cow. I don't know why they do it, in the prime of life, everything still pert and perky. Fucking shame.

Some of them do it for the social, sure, but most of these teen pregnancies, they're all about the necessary. The girls will tell you it's about the love, but it's about the fucking. The speccy twats off the box make out that fucking and love are the same thing, that these dames are filling a gap. They're not.

Tracy-May was a mistake waiting to happen. Skinny as fuck but with these great, wide hips inviting you in, offering maternal refuge. Christ, we'd all had a go. All sunk our fingers into those soft handles and imagined her blooming with our seed. Always appreciative, Tracy-May. Always willing to please. Fuck. She's out of the game now – it'll take her years to get that figure back, if she ever does. Fucking shame.

Still, there's always the hope, the slim chance that she

won't drop out of the game just yet, that she'll welcome a little more attention. Christ, have you ever had a go on a woman who's ripening and ready to balloon? Oh pal, you've gotta try it. The bulging breasts, the ultra-sensitive nipples – but don't think that's the main event, oh no. Bend one of these aching mothers-to-be over and give it one from behind, reaching round to feel the swelling of new life groaning as you disturb the peace. Corrupt them early, see, let them know what's to come. It's the perfect marriage of the symbolic and the sensual. Fuck.

And you know what's worse than seeing a tight young broad brutalised over nine months – permanently disfigured? It's seeing the slack-jawed dickweed who's inflicted the punishment on her. The greasy-haired, semi-literate twat who's done the duty. Jesus, how does it happen? You'd have to be pretty fucking wasted to let that anywhere near your intimates – if the wrapping is as unappealing as that, imagine what the package is like, not to mention the discharge. Christ.

Still, Tracy-May isn't the first and she won't be the last. It's just one less cunt in the sea, I guess. Fucking shame.

* * * *

The buzz of unseen activity – motors roaring, people chattering – it's the soundtrack we no longer notice. Silence is a long forgotten idea; nowadays, we're all perfectly adept at tuning out, tuning in, choosing the channels that scream loud enough to be worth listening to.

People, they don't understand how oppressive true silence is. It's an idyll that they've never experienced. True silence twangs like a violin string tightened too far, like the gasp of dying souls fading into the abyss. It's anxiety, it's razor sharp. No, silence is not what we crave. There's comfort in the familiar hum of activity – it provides an anonymity that silence just doesn't allow.

Sitting here on this bench, I can see nothing but buildings all around – no people, no cars, and yet I know they're there – the sound, when sought out, reminds me that I'm not alone, that this is a reality where industry continues around me with or without my input. It's empowering – the knowledge that all these fucking lemmings continue on through their blinkered lives while the few, like me, can just take it all in, enjoy being lost in the swirl of their effort, without being a part of it. I'm an observer, someone who truly knows what's going on.

The greyness of the world – the sky, the buildings, the roads and pavements – it's the perfect tone of comfort, away from the penetrating, sterile whites or deep, fearful blacks. It's the mid-tone that anaesthetises, fights off the anxiety and allows the lemmings to continue in their daily business without confronting their true natures. It's a brilliant collusion on the part of architects and town planners.

Course, now they're using all this glass, which reflects back the greyness, but with a small addition – you – yeah, you're part of the architecture. Slope past one of these great, glass-covered blocks and your reflection is the only thing that breaks the mid-tone pallor. It's the perfect design feature – you're centre stage, shining out from the limp background, vibrant and exotic. People lap that shit up – their own image following them around the world, no longer necessary to seek it out, but instead surrounded by it, pursued by it. Narcissism isn't an option anymore; without it you just wouldn't survive the show.

No tower block mirrors round here though – this little square isn't part of the modern; it's retrograde, still pulling itself into the future. Stone and metal – not warm or cold – is comforting in its familiarity. The windows grimy, you'd be lucky to find any kind of reflection in them. Take a look – you won't be in high-definition, my friend. Go right ahead, you'll not show up as more than an indefinite blur here – this is the past, the age of the masses – we don't tolerate that shit anymore, we demand the individual these days, absolutely require the crisp, clear-eyed clarity of our image, our self.

The wind blows a few scattered leaves across the square – fuck knows which tree they came from, because there's nothing living in sight. They graze the concrete of the road silently, their whispered connection drowned out by the background noise.

Rocking my head back, I look up to the top of the building almost directly in front of me – its meagre five stories tell the world that it's a relic, dwarfed many times over by the fresh, vigorous developments that press up towards the heavens. This is a quiet part of town, never at the cutting edge, now all but forgotten. Plastic spikes jut out from every ledge and balcony – life isn't welcome here – but the pebble dash is smeared with bird shit; a reminder that life persists, even in the face of hostility.

Small stones are set into the concrete walls, and, as I watch, some fall loose – a liberation decades in the making – a quiet twist in the moveless reality of the square. Soft clacks as the stones hit the pavement below confirm their final dive to freedom.

The few stones, now detached, become part of the debris that covers the ground wherever you go in this part of town. There's little effort to move things on, to demand that only the fresh survive. After their fall, the stones won't go anywhere quickly, their descent halted, their escape stalled. They're destined to remain in the shadow of their oppressor.

More clacks as unseen stones follow their brothers, a heavy rain of rebellion falling now. I try to focus my eyes, try to find the source, but all is lost in the weight of the rain, the rolling cracks of noise as hardness meets hardness. Amongst the tides of sound, a deep vibration penetrates as something heavier makes the downward journey.

Looking up, I can just make out the tops of the buildings, now falling to earth as the tower blocks sink inwards, collapsing over and slowly releasing debris as they struggle to maintain balance. It's too late; the inevitable crash is moments away.

* * * *

Lexi's flight touches down in 72 hours exactly. Soon, those bra-busting beauties will be back on these shores and back within fondling distance. Christ, I'm ready to fall back into the routine: dirty Thursdays – the full package, the whole orchestra; and Sundays, always quieter. A quickie after evening mass for my little Catholic nympho. Doesn't that get you off – imagining Lexi on her knees, those tight lips pursed around a prayer? It's the ultimate form of submission, the perfect bondage. No wonder the priests are all kiddy-fiddlers or sado-fuckers. An orgy of submission once a week just isn't enough for these hungry cunts. And who can blame them? I'd have Lexi on her knees at every opportunity if all I had to do was throw a few Hail Mary's about the place. Fuck.

Listen, now don't go thinking I'm a bender or a nancy, but I wanted to do something for Lexi, to welcome her back into the country. I'm not into that weepy shit at the airport – the phony tears, the reserve barely thrown off. No. Besides, Lex won't want me to see her after a 10-hour flight, when she's all mushed up and in a state. Christ, that wouldn't do either of us any good. She's got her standards to maintain; if the illusion drops then all bets are off. So no, an airport reunion is out of the question for this horny fucker. Instead, I'm going to write her a little note, a little welcome back message. Short, to the point. She'll like it. It'll pay dividends.

But don't go thinking this is one of those fancy

affairs, my friend, no wax-sealed envelopes or flowery poems in these parts, pal. Balls to that - who needs it? No, your standard lined sheet torn from my trusty pad will do the trick. Bum an envelope off Mum, pop in the note, a quick snap of Mr. Happy to whet the appetite, and down to the post office to get this show on the road.

It's the digital age they tell you, reality is dead. They're not far wrong, but you've got to know how to use reality, how to turn it to your advantage. See, I know there'll be plenty of fuckers who're packing a hard-on for Lexi – she's not shy about sharing the love – but what will all these other dickweeds do? Wait until they see her next? Send her a text, or an e-mail? That's why I stand out, that's why we're the real deal. I see beyond that shit, understand the need for touch, the need to connect. You can't feel an e-mail against your skin, can't weigh it in your hands and hold it close to your bulging bosom.

It's a load of bollocks, I know; a bad advert, a sentimental twinge for a sentiment that never existed in the first place. But that doesn't mean it's not useful. It doesn't mean that Lexi won't fall for it hook, line, and sink 'er - she's only human, she can't help but give in to the myth, if only a little.

* * * *

This is hot, too hot – I didn't expect it. I'm sweating and aching, moving slowly towards the finishing line, the climax to this tawdry affair. It's a total ball ache.

This fat bird in front of me offers no distraction, her giant ass jutting out from her thick back. A bead of sweat trickles down her neck, losing itself amongst the rolls of fat. I sigh. She looks round, disdain on her face. I move closer, glare back at her. We're in this together, there is no fast-forward button, no skipping to the money-shot. My legs ache, my back aches. I breathe heavily and steal another inch, want her to really feel it, acknowledge my presence. She lets out a sharp sigh, more dismissive than surprised.

There are similarly clipped gasps from others too – no one's at their best. I can sense someone coming up behind me – a pretty dame, I hope. Something to pass the time, ignite a little something in this stifling room, kept in half-light. I turn. A great cupboard of a man stops short. Entwined with his greying chest hair, the chain of his medallion falls at my eye level. I don't register his face but turn back. The lumpy dame has widened the gap between us, I drive forward, determined to make every inch count.

She turns her head again, eyes me coldly. But her gaze continues, goes past me and to this bloke behind, the new member of our little dance.

"Hello, Trev. You alright, darling?" she calls over my head.

"Not bad, love, didn't expect to see you here. Thought you were off down the in-laws this week?"

Fucking rude; talking over me. What a pair of twats.

"Oh no, Steve's got a job on."

This lumbering wanker is edging round now, almost

at my shoulder. I stare ahead, focus on the task at hand.

"Has he, love? Big one, is it?"

This guy reeks. A great, big, musty stink.

"Oh, Steve hasn't had a big one for years," she half-smirks.

"Yeah, I've heard."

Fatty swings round and belts him one on the arm, "Cheeky sod!"

They laugh. I look straight ahead, hips rocking gently now.

"Eh, you know where to come if you want a big one, love," he says, winking at her and nudging my arm, "Eh, kid?" as he looks down at me.

I glance up at him, his foul moustache flecked with saliva, or sweat, or both. If I had my screwdriver to hand, fuck, straight into his bloated stomach. Drive it deep into that gluttonous cunt.

I look forward. Fatty rolls her eyes. Pliers for her, I think. Clamped hard around the sow's great sagging udders. Rip her nipples clean away. Fucking smirk at me then, you stupid cunt.

This hulking twat motions with his head, "Eh, do you mind, mate?" as he steps in front of me.

I shrug, withdraw. Hope he has better luck than me, hope it's over quickly.

His buttocks strain, bulging in my direction, and his broad back covers my vision. I tune out, I don't need this shit.

I flex my right hand, longing for the touch of cold metal on my skin, longing to have something to drive deep into the mound of flesh in front of me.

I look down, realise I've screwed up Lexi's letter. I sigh. The cashier calls the next customer to the desk. We shuffle forward – perfect social order maintained.

* * * *

Knowledge is power, that's what they say. Course, nowadays, knowledge is everyone's – maybe we're all empowered, or maybe we're drowning in a reality we'd rather ignore. Fact is though, it's all out there, at your fingertips, waiting to be put to good use. Ignorance isn't an option anymore – the only decision is what to do with the information thrust upon you.

The laptop springs to life, and the comforting whirr sends me hurtling towards truth; salvation awaits for some, condemnation for others. I grab my phone and skim through the basic information I've gleaned so far: Annabel Bird, in her thirties, unmarried, psychiatrist, studied at University of Sheffield. It's more than enough information to crack open her online footprint, to learn everything there is to know about Ms. Bird. You might say she's been vacant to let that much slip, but you can't contend anymore, privacy doesn't exist no matter how much you'd like to think it does. Fucking mugs shred every piece of paper that mentions even half their address, when everything you could ever want to know – bank details to medical history – is all out there, online, in the world, freely available. It's just a fact; this is the world we live in.

Computer loaded, I begin my own investigation.

Within two minutes I have a full C.V. for Annabel, including work and education history. It doesn't make for interesting reading, doesn't show up much you couldn't have guessed anyway: average grades, decent schools, pill-pushing jobs since she was in her twenties. It's a predictable life, a predictable trajectory. Doesn't that get you? All this information available 24/7 – the full deets on any dame or cock-slinger you like – and when it comes down to it, the tawdry mundane reins. People are predictable, they're all shades of grey with little to break up the dreary reality of their existence. Quantified, recorded, their lives amount to little. They're easily pigeon-holed, pushed into one category or another and then ignored for the rest of their lives until they reach the inevitable end of their trajectory. Fucking tedious.

I go further, pull up some papers Bird wrote when she was still bright-eyed and fresh out of uni: more predictability. Her peers didn't make much of her; a few small-time publications, nothing worth writing home about. It's all here, scored, rated, rejected in a few clicks. Unexceptional.

Now for the real stuff: the personal. I call up as many social profiles as possible, flicking through the same bare information, same small collection of photographs. Even within the confines of her online identity, Annabel struggles to breathe, the staleness apparent across all her online activity. You've got to wonder at the point to social profiles for these people, the ones who barely exist as three-dimensional people, let alone in the flattening, fattening space of digital reality.

The final stone upturned: a dating profile. Now here's something that's had a little care. Just the one photo mind: plain, but truthful. Annabel stares out at the camera, a weak smile barely hiding her awkwardness as she sits in some fancy bar, presumably with a friend, wine glasses and empty plates sitting in front of her. I enlarge the image, searching for some further spark of life but find none. It's a photo of an Annabel past, but not so far back as to offer any hope of a life more interesting.

I scroll down, find what she's searching for in a man: kind, professional, enjoys walking. All the normal bollocks. They really are simple, women. At least, they are when they don't have enough to offer to make any real demands. Annabel, she's a professional woman, healthy and secure. There's little more to say, and there's little more she wants in return. It's a pretty simple matching process, the coupling of the equally dull. You'd almost feel sorry for the fucking saps if they didn't bring it on themselves. But then that's the predictable, that's life.

* * * *

The heavy heat weighs in on me, filling my lungs and sticking in my nostrils. The prickle of summer hits me in waves, and I glare down at the pavement, which only reflects back the hideous heat bearing in from above. Unseen kids scream, and the world reclines. No one goes full steam in summer.

Happy cunts fly along the streets, results papers clutched in their hands; proud of their achievements, relieved to have been assured of making the next step on their path to anonymity, to conformity. They're all happy for now, all full of the euphoria of tension released. Somewhere, the couples will be fucking, their result slips discarded on the floors of their bedrooms, while clammy hands explore new territories. Others will be surrounded by doting parents, who celebrate with their deluded offspring, glad that everything remains 'normal', 'on course'.

The chime of an ice cream van sounds. It can't be more than a few streets away, and a couple of tentative heads poke from flung-open windows, looking out for the trundling van. Keep looking, there's nothing to see here.

A car horn cuts through the stagnant air as a small Renault, packed with college kids, rushes by, throwing loose stones into the air. I barely look up before the car has passed, dwindling into the distance before the brake lights erupt into life at the junction. There's nothing to see here.

A skinny girl in crop-top and oversized sunglasses rolls her scooter across the road, her brown legs carrying her faster than they have any right to. Another girl, thicker around the waist and without shape, follows. Her face a half-scowl, she's not making the most of the school holidays. Perhaps she's just a grump, perhaps she's mixing with the wrong crowd.

My eyes sting as the light becomes too much and salty tears blur the world around me. I blink them away, keep my head down and my eyes on the pavement. They sting all the same. Fucking typical.

I cross the threshold into my own space, the crack in the concrete a boundary ill-defined. My knuckle lightly grazes the hinge that used to hold a gate. I'm through the door and almost at the stairs when Mum calls out:

"How did it go?"

I don't reply – what can you say? But she's bridged the gap between us, emerged from the living room, remote in hand, "So?"

I thrust the crumpled paper from my hand to hers. She surveys it, no readable expression on her face. "Oh well, love."

She takes a step forward, but I retreat onto the stairs. That emotional bollocks isn't needed here. A hug doesn't change the grades on the paper.

"Maybe you can get into a different uni still?" she offers.

"No," I say, turning to head up the stairs.

The front door opens once more and Dad stalks in.

"Alright, soppy bollocks, how'd it go?"

Mum offers up the paper, "Here are, Mick."

He looks at it for a minute, "So what's this mean?" he asks.

"No uni," Mum says.

"Dopey cunt," Dad grins, "You don't need all that education anyway – mug's game."

Mum rolls her eyes and I make the definite movement

away from it all, up the stairs and into my own space. There's nothing to see here.

As I go I hear Dad demanding, "What?"

I don't hear the response, but the smack of skin on flesh and the muffled yelp tell me it wasn't the right answer. Dopey cunt, it's never the right answer.

* * * *

My instant messenger beeps.

"Hey :)"

Chloe's avatar appears in the bottom right of my screen.

"…"

I load up a new page, search 'Skinny goth, big natural tits'

"Whatcha upto?"

Double Ds burst across the screen, pale chicks with soft bodies. Some with tattoos, others with piercings.

"…"

Most aren't really skinny, not Chloe skinny anyway. But then it's rare to get a proper slim bird with decent knockers.

"Free 2 chat?"

I click on a particularly well-endowed broad with no hips and even less waist. This slut erupts at the ribcage, huge bulging breasts exploding out towards the camera. Fake. Not the tits, the image. Probably a trick of the camera lens, maybe post-production. No one has a body like that.

"Helloooooo?"

I hate the fake images. I hate having to work out what's real and what's not. Some days I just relax into it, accept the fantasy. Others, well, I can't accept the lie, can't buy in to the illusion. Every day they get a little better at distorting reality. If it's not bras stuffed with all sorts of filler, it's the surgeon's knife. And then there's all the camera tricks: angles, lens, computer distortions. You can't trust a thing. Video, that's about as real as it comes.

"?????"

This busty goth, she's got natural bangers I reckon, but that's as far as I'd go – the rest is debatable, is down to your own imagination. And that's the thing; it's what you can do with your mind, what they can make you believe. Me, I'm undecided, I'm in the country between faith and the lies.

":(x"

I close my instant messenger and fire up a video of this tasty Goth. Reality awaits.

* * * *

The sweet, spreading heat – pain erupting from a small patch in the centre of my forehead. The muscles in my neck tense, the twinge of a well-rehearsed reaction. My head speeds through the six inches of heavy air and smacks, sweet as a nut, into my target. Blind for a moment, I pull back as the nerves tingle again. It's a practiced art – meeting your target, inflicting as little damage on yourself as possible, dealing with the inevitable pain. And that's the thing, fighting is about pain – it sounds obvious – but most guys, well they think it's all about landing the knockout blow. It's not. It's about sticking in there, taking the punches and not giving in to the sickness in your stomach. That's what fighting's about: toleration. Like life, those who can put up with the most invariably come out on top. So you've got to train yourself to take the pain, dull the senses enough that you can take it all, smilingly.

A deep breath and I strike again. Pulling back, I watch as the world swims momentarily and then settles into sharp reality. The splintered crack in the cream plaster runs right through the inked bullseye, testament to the accuracy and power of my delivery.

Turning, I pick a pair of fingerless leather gloves up from my bed, and pull them over my knuckles. Returning to the wall, I re-focus my energy, clench my fists, and picture going through the wall. Drawing back my right hand I drive the knuckle into the target; sharp, accurate, it kisses the surface. I repeat the same with my left, then wriggle my fingers, loosening the whole hand. Another deep breath and I send a volley of ferocious punches against the target, all find their range, the padding of the gloves hardly compressing on each shot. It helps to have cultured hands when you're an urban baby, when survival and violence are the same thing.

Standing closer in, I eye up the target, give it the stare before shooting my right hand through in an uppercut, followed swiftly by the left. Fighters have to be ambidextrous. It doesn't matter where the attack is coming from, you've got to be able to cover it. And not just with your hands, your feet have got to be equally lethal.

Stretching my quads, I limber up for some kicks – less controlled, but more powerful, they're something a little different. Most people, see, they follow the fists, but not many expect a kick to smash into their jaw and take them out. Element of surprise.

Muscles loose, I start with a few spinning heel kicks in the middle of the room. It's hard in the contained space, but you've got to be able to fight in all sorts of environments. Occasionally, my heel will clip the bed, send the mattress shooting across the smooth boards and onto the floor. It's reassuring to know the power is there, but I'm still reining in the control. No spills this morning, and I get the target in my sights once more: standing swipe kicks, followed by full-extension front kicks. Deep breath and–

"Give it a rest!" Mum's voice cuts through the air from the living room.

I pound the wall with a defiant punch.

"Oi!"

Silly cow. I check my breathing, feel the warm tension in muscles. I've done enough. Stripping off my gloves, I collapse back onto the bed. Practice can wait.

* * * *

"How've you been this week?"

I stand out of my chair and walk to the cluttered desk that rests against the wall of the office, a filing place and nothing more. Pushing the piles of paper about, I sit on the mean gap I've created.

Annabel looks confused.

"What are we doing?"

Well, darling, I don't know about you, but I'm changing things up a little. I give her the look, and breathe deeply.

She stands, unsure what happens next.

I only smile as she slowly edges across the carpet, which crackles with static electricity, to where I sit.

"What are we doing?" She repeats the question. In answer I grab her right wrist and press her hand into my lap, to where my heavy erection bulges against my jeans.

"Oh," she stammers.

I grin and pull my jeans and pants down in one smooth movement. Her eyes widen and I force her head down, my fingers firm amongst her dry hair.

* * * *

Row upon row of shining treats gleam out from the vending machine's hard casing, each screaming for attention, calling you to hit the button and release them from their crowded prison. One by one they've watched their comrades liberated, sent into the world to be enjoyed. A small fall to freedom, they all long to fling themselves to the same fate, like bodies falling to the earth before the second plane. They seek only a release, a leap towards the inevitable.

My finger hovers over the keypad, money already

safely inserted – I'm committed, but now paralysed by the choice, made euphoric and anxious by all the metallic colours glistening in front of me: reds, purples, greens, blues. It's too much. There's no way to narrow the options. For a moment, I consider walking away, leaving the machine on the cusp of ejaculation, abandoning the small deposit for the next lucky visitor to this game where everyone wins.

But I don't. I stay; I'm part of the game now, walking away isn't an option, not really. In a world of choice the only logical option is to leave it to chance. And so I do. Closing my eyes momentarily, and punching two numbers at random, I assert my selection.

Poised with a new anticipation, I wait to see which of the metal coils will unwind and allow one of its captives to escape to the pit below. Slowly, number 43 begins to move – I watch eagerly as the smooth metal rumples the chocolate's wrapper – just a few more millimetres, just one or two. And then number 42 begins to move too. And 37. Then 23. 56. 27. The crackle and plop of the wrappers colliding as they fight to enjoy gravity's pull is hideous, a scat wall of sound. Hundreds of bodies flinging themselves from buildings now, the sea of the fallen overflowing below.

* * * *

The smell of burning dust surrounds me, the library's radiators on full blast to fight away the chill outside. The atmosphere pregnant with the expectation of noise, everyone is poised to stop, to glare; everyone living in expectation of a moment to come. Inevitably, it does.

Some daft lads come clunking through the front door, letting the outside world seep in before the door bangs back into place. Everyone inside looks up; a disturbance anticipated. Eyes roll and tongues cluck, and everyone goes back to a state of nervous expectancy. This is how we live now.

The librarians used to 'shh' and shoo people around the place – not anymore. We live in a self-policing state now; everyone understands the limits of their role or their ability to rebel. These lads, they've fallen straight into line, no questions asked: they're shuffling about, looking for a place to set themselves down, to join the majority.

The clitter clatter of fingers dancing over keyboards irritates the brain. The stink of the guy next to me – a library regular – gets into my senses, mixes with the comforting smell of the bookshelves. It's too much – what sort of prick comes out reeking like this? Someone needs to have a word, explain that we've moved beyond the days of cavemen, that you're allowed to slap on a bit of deodorant. Raggedy clothes and hair all over the place too: fucking Neanderthal. Doesn't he have a mirror? Doesn't he have a fucking woman to explain this shit to him? Hell, you don't even need a woman anymore – the world's at the end of your fingertips, at the end of his right now. Take a couple of minutes, get an opinion, read an article. Christ. Some people have just fallen so far out of reality they can barely count themselves as part of the same species any more.

I look over at his screen: a scrawling line tracks the fortunes of some stock or other. He glances sideways then looks back at the screen, "Up two points today. That's good. Mark says they're going to go up at least ten by the end of the week," he sniffs. "I bought a hundred and fifty pounds last week. Easy money."

Course you have, mate – we all play the stock market down here. Fucking mug.

He flicks between windows: 'GetConnected: Earn $1,000/week from home'.

"This is the one, here. You sign up and get a website, then you get five dollars every time you recommend a friend to the scheme too. See?"

I watch as he traces a diagram with the cursor, "And then when they refer someone you get another five. See?" The diagram expands, tiny digital people on top of other digital people. One at the pinnacle – you – standing on top of hundreds, all working together, all making you money. You, the top of the food chain, creaming the system, building up your earnings. "Do you see?" he says again.

I nod, "Mmm."

His voice skitters off again, tripping over each sentence to get to the next: "I only signed up last week. Here." He brings up a page which details his 'network'. "You see? It keeps track of everyone I sign up, here. Let's me know when they've paid their seventy-five dollars to join, and then I get my five dollars."

I run my eyes over the page – over this fucking slob's profile, his grainy profile picture: same hairstyle, same grime, forced smile.

"So that's your network?" I ask, looking at the one solitary name.

"Yeah. I've got one already, and I only signed up last week. Do you see?"

I do see. "Who's Brad?"

"He works for GetConnected – he's my agent. They always make sure 'newbies' have an agent – so they're not alone. Look." He pulls up Brad's profile – a gleaming smile, health radiating from his smooth tan, an open-necked shirt revealing the top of a chiselled American chest. The sort of chest only an American has: puffed up, preened – a poser's chest. "He's already given me some really good tips – I'm just trying things out at the moment, then I'm going to start up properly. Brad says I can sign up for another account – it's kind of against the rules, but he says he's 'got my back' – and then I can have this other account in my network, so anytime I sign someone up for an account I get rewards on both accounts. See? So it's only another seventy-five dollars, but then I double my earning power. It's all about leveraging your earning potential, see?"

He brings up another page. Glossy Americans in a sports car race across the screen – Barbie and Ken – heading back to their mansion, built on the dollars of schemes like this. "Do you see?"

I sigh, "Yeah." Turning back to my screen, I thrust headphones into my ears. There's no music, but they do their job. The stinking entrepreneur goes back to examining his 'network'. I ram my USB into the tired library PC – at least five years out of date – and browse the photos stored on the stick.

Images of Lexi flash across the screen – PG-13 for the most part. I flick through, looking for the one of her in that tight sky-blue sweater, her cleavage bursting from the low-cut v. I can feel the stale breath of my neighbour brushing the side of my face. I stare straight ahead, but he nudges me:

"She's nice."

"Mm." I nod and hide the window, not wanting this grubby bastard getting a stiffy off my girlfriend. No fucking boundaries, these filth-mongers.

An alert flashes across his screen and he rushes off to the helpdesk in search of a librarian to extend his computer time before he's disconnected, cut adrift from the world.

I pull up the picture I'm looking for and hit 'Print' before the pervert returns. Yanking my USB from the computer, I log off.

Walking past shelf after shelf of untouched books, I make my way to the helpdesk. Students and sad bastards hide amongst the stacks, idling away their day.

At the desk, I join the queue for printing and watch as the librarian exchanges money for scraps of paper: reproductions of a digital reality not meant to find a physical medium.

The librarian barks to beckon forward the next customer, who laces her palm with a handful of coins, before her stout frame waddles off to grab the freshly printed pages from the old printer, which clunks away beneath the desk. I edge forward, two 10 pence coins clasped tightly in my hand.

When the queue clears, I step up to the desk and drop my library card and the two coins – warm now – onto the counter. The librarian scoops them up and shuffles off on her much travelled path; I lean heavily on the desk. As she bends to retrieve Lexi I hear complaints from the printer, the scrunch of paper as it grinds to a halt. The librarian hands me a half-printed version of Lexi and one of my coins back, "It jammed."

I look down at the page; below Lex's shoulders the colour fades into the white page, beauty stalled, interrupted. I tear away the blank paper, clearing the void until the image is cropped close to Lexi's face and the tip of her shoulders: a perfect headshot. I slip the picture into my wallet and walk out.

* * * *

"Ready?"

A deep, growling voice wakes me. Lazily, I pull my eyes open but am met with more darkness. Fucking ball ache – the middle of the night is no time to be woken for anything less than a banging slut.

"Ready?" The gruff voice repeats itself, and I search out its owner. At my feet a shadowy figure moves, all features but one obscured: in his right hand there's the glint of metal, a shining blade the only thing visible in the blackness.

I try to sit up, to engage with this presence, to explain that this is not the fucking time, but I can't.

My muscles tense but my body doesn't respond – I'm paralysed, restrained, a spectator.

"Easy now," the voice says. Stepping forward, the shadow makes its way up the side of the bed and towards my face. A large palm reaches out and covers my face, my vision completely obscured once more.

"Relax – I'm just going to take a couple of small things," the voice reassures.

I try to protest, to demand explanation, but my vocal chords are as frozen as the rest of me. Blind, I feel the shadow moving over my body and reaching down to my naked crotch.

"Don't worry – you won't miss these."

* * * *

I never really understood why all the soppy cunts had to surround themselves with images of their squeezes. I mean, fine, it's something to look at, isn't it? But really, you've got more than enough chance to look at them in the flesh, no? Every fucking night while you're doing it in all three dimensions. So why the need to have that image follow you around everywhere, why not take up some of the variety that the world has to offer? Give your eyes something to keep them bright and hungry for the world? And let's be honest, most of the dames these dickweeds fawn over are pretty standard stuff, at best. Just because you have to settle for that in the sack, doesn't mean you can't enjoy yourself outside the necessary.

Lately, though, I've been thinking there's something

to it. Ok, Lex is a long way ahead of your average steady Betty, but even still, I've always kinda figured variety is what makes life worth living, right? The minute you stop, commit, make one point the steady centre of your world, you might as well give up. But actually, well, maybe there's something to it. I mean, Lex has been on permanent loop in my head for weeks, so what's the difference in taking the internal and making it a little more solid? And who wouldn't want a fine piece like Lexi everywhere they looked anyway? Fuck, surrounding yourself with that sort of image only keeps you on it, keeps lead in the pencil at all times.

Check this one out here – come on now, I don't mind sharing – look at the shape of her figure, the smooth line running over her hips and creating a perfect curve with those bangers. That's hardly the ordinary, is it? Lexi is a worthy successor to Kim Kardashian on the laptop's background.

Pull all the icons away from her perfect frame, keep her unblemished and visible at a click of the button. Yes, my friend, it ain't so bad, this. I can see that there's something to it.

"Oi, herbert. Where's your ma?"

My room's door cracks off the wardrobe, Dad's hand holds it in place.

"What the fuck are you doing here?"

"Charming, that. Where's the old hag?" Dad says.

"Dunno."

She's probably down the social club, but how the fuck can I say – I don't keep tabs on what every other fucker is doing.

"Down the bingo, is it?" he says.

"What do you want her for?"

"Nothing."

It's a lot of fuss for nothing. Particularly when that nothing will almost certainly end in a barney.

Dad steps into the room, his heavy boots barely scuffing the surface of the carpet as he moves. "Oh, like her, do ya?" he says, nodding at the laptop.

I snap the screen shut, hiding Lexi's shame.

"Good taste, lad. She's definitely one in the wank bank."

"Mm," I say, looking down as Dad rearranges his balls through his jeans.

Looking around, he sniffs, "Some of her flicks are fucking top – proper porno, right?"

"Mm."

"Something for you to dream about anyway, eh, virgin? Wouldn't mind popping it with someone like her, would ya, you scrawny fucker?"

The sandpaper rough skin of his palm irritates as Dad grasps me at the base of my neck, shaking my senses. He doesn't get it; not really. But how could he? Every day he falls further behind, his day fading into the distance as my star rises.

"Come on; let's get a pint, soppy bollocks."

"Why?" I ask.

"Fuck off."

"Where's Casey?" I ask.

"Oh, like another look at that cunt's jelly arse, would

ya?" he says, grabbing my cheek roughly. "Come on, it's just the lads tonight – who needs snatch to have a good time, right?"

Pulling me up, he's halfway to the door before I can grab my coat. Lad's night out it is.

* * * *

It's physical – the ache of boredom that you get from the lost hours. My shoulders, my back - all is stiff, paralysed from the stillness. Annabel Bird behind me, I'm back into my world, the world where no one asks questions, where no one has time for answers. It's liberation; it's that loosening in the chest. When you can get on with the life you're living without intrusion, without enquiry, that's freedom. There's no sense trying to connect - we don't know how anymore, empathy is a foreign language and we're all the better for it. People still fumble their way through interactions of course, kid themselves that they're mastering the art. The old school. You and me, we know what it's all about, don't we? You have to let these things pass: it's evolution, it's revolution.

All those at the mental health clinic, they all have a crack: makes me fucking sick, makes my skin crawl. Annabel Bird is one thing, but the sows on reception – Jesus. They're there to answer phones and buzz doors – what business do they have trying to empathise? They'll do it though, as you walk in, as you walk out, the same false smile, the one that says 'good on you, son', 'stiff upper lip, you'll get through this', 'you're alright' – but it's all an act. Who is ok these days? And who cares? I'm not alright, they're not alright, none of us are alright, so why waste any of your energy on someone else's problems? And that's what makes my skin crawl – the sham of empathy. A smile is just the contortion of a face – it's meaningless, there's nothing behind it. Yet, people will kid themselves that it's enough, that they're making the world a better place. No, my friend, we know the truth. It's authenticity, isn't it? I don't give a fuck about you and you don't give a fuck about me, so why pretend any different? It doesn't do. It's the ultimate cruelty.

* * * *

I wipe the grime and sweat from my forehead – a hard day's work. Promised I'd chat with Chloe tonight – full video, the whole shebang. Reckons I don't pay her enough attention, dozy mare. They're all the same, women, absolutely gagging for your attention – all of it. How they think they can command that much attention, deserve that much focused energy, I don't know. There's too much going on out there, too many minds and bodies to connect with. Taking all that attention – demanding it – things just don't work that way, not anymore.

A quick look at my contacts and I see Chloe's online – of course she's online. She's plugged in, part of the new age.

"Hey."

My instant messenger has barely loaded and she's

already invading my personal space – that's the thing about Chloe these days, she doesn't give you room to breathe, room to settle. Claustrophobia, it doesn't get girls the way it does guys – they crave that connection, that sense of shared experience. Guys, we need our space, understand that we live independently.

"Hey." I accept the video chat request and Chloe's image flickers in front of me. Everything is pale, the soft light casting shadows across her face. No make-up, lazy bitch. She looks tired.

"How's your day been?"

It's a loaded question – she wants to know, wants a proper answer. But you can't go overboard – she doesn't want every detail, she only wants to know that you want to tell her. What she actually wants is the question reflected back at her, wants to be given the floor to unleash her own personal story, to take centre stage like everyone else. Even with intimates, we don't communicate, we speak.

"Yeah, alright. Been down the library doing some research."

That's all she wants to hear – you can't give girls too much, can't let them in on your real life, only your acceptable one.

"Cool. Whatcha researching?"

I sigh, and pull a copy of Plato's *Republic* in front of the camera. She juts her bottom lip up and shrugs her shoulders. I throw the book onto my chair and look back.

"So, I wanted to talk, you know, properly," she says.

Fuck me, do girls ever give over? They'll never talk themselves dry – when they run out of things to say, they just start over, running through the same old things, seeking reassurance, confirmation.

"Yeah?"

I sink back onto my pillow, which is propped up at the end of my bed. This is going to be one of those nights.

"Yeah. We don't talk enough – we used to talk. I was thinking about that today."

The warm underbelly of my laptop rests snuggly on my lap. I can feel the processors humming away, reassuring. The weight of the unit pressing on my crotch gets the juices flowing; I feel the blood rush and the familiar stirring.

"Oh yeah?" I say.

Chloe is looking pale today – even for her anaemic self. The veins on her chest trace the life force that courses weakly through her body, pressing up towards her frail, paper-thin skin.

"You don't notice – when we don't talk so much?"

I wonder if the veins snake their way down to Chloe's cherry-ripe nipples, whether those perky pointers are at the eye of the electric storm of veins raging around them.

"I suppose."

"Really? Because sometimes it feels like you don't. And it does matter, doesn't it?"

I shift the laptop forward up my belly as the swelling in my pants becomes uncomfortable under the weight.

Chloe crooks a smile with the corner of her mouth and pulls her laptop closer too. Her tits almost fall out of shot, but the camera settles just right. Reaching down, I rub my bulging jeans and imagine sinking my teeth into those frigid B cups.

"Yeah, I guess so."

With my other hand, I slip my phone out of my pocket and search the internet for "veiny tits".

"Ok, because sometimes I feel like you don't see me. Like I'm invisible."

If she gets much paler she will be. Christ, she picks her moments.

"You're not invisible."

A pair of great sagging breasts riddled with veins pops up. Not quite what we need here. I continue flicking through results.

"It hurts."

Soppy bullshit. Emotional guilt-tripping. Why does it always come down to this with women? Why can't they take responsibility for their own miserable emotions and stop putting it on those of us who are trying to actually get something out of this world?

"Yeah."

Perfect. Pretty pointers with veins dancing around the protruding nipples. Pert, tasty - just what's required. I slide my jeans down and get hold of the serious bit of meat that's grown up between my legs.

The words have stopped; I look up. Chloe's mouth is pinched, her eyes misty. Fuck sake.

"What?" I say, exasperated.

I can feel the thick shaft of my cock, my own veins bursting forward now.

"It hurts."

You wanna calm down, love. A good cock up your arse, that hurts. That'd make your eyes water. All this emotional bollocks, no, get it together – it's not worth the agitation.

I slide my finger across the phone's screen, zoom in on the nipple, the soft pink flesh.

"Why won't you make it better?"

Christ, what can you do for people like this? I slide the laptop down my belly until it reaches the hump of my erection.

"Wanna see something that'll cheer you up?"

"Make it better," she says, ignoring the question.

I pause, let my dick loll to one side.

"Huh?"

Chloe pushes the laptop away, and looks down at her lap. I look down too. Sticky blood stains her wrists and bed clothes.

"It hurts."

* * * *

Did you know the electric chair was invented by a dentist? How about this one: the first bomb dropped on Germany during World War II killed the only elephant in Berlin Zoo? There are no clocks in Las Vegas casinos. Napoleon's penis was dismembered and sold to an American urologist. The human heart creates enough blood to squirt blood thirty feet.

* * * *

The heavy, dank smell of cut grass seeps into my senses. I drink it in, its clear, simple texture unfamiliar, unwanted. Looking down the hill I can see reality, existing without me. Streets cut a path through the indifferent buildings that divide the cityscape, isolate the citizens. The city wakes, it lives. Out here all is decay: the fields, the trees, the earth – it's a poem to a forgotten world. It's retrograde, untenable, unbearable. One day we'll cut through it in swathes, clear the Earth of the past and truly move to the future. Brush aside the sentimentality and look forward instead of ever back.

The soft fibres of the picnic rug beneath my fingers bristles, ill at ease in its surroundings. I look at the selection of bite-sized foods set out across the rug, cling-film balls stuck to plates. There's a crumpled gap where Lexi's firm buttocks have borne into the ground, pressing the synthetic rug into the authentic earth. I reach across, straighten the rug, feeling the warmth it retains.

Lexi looks fine today. A polka dot dress held in at the waist by a red plastic belt. God, what a figure! Her hair curled, and falling about her shoulders in a wonderfully classic style. She's a 50s goddess, an icon, an idol. She's untameable, unbearable, but she's mine.

I hear the crack of twigs as she approaches from behind, close my eyes and feel the warm prickles of pleasure swarm up my back and through my neck; the pleasurable lightness of her return. Her soft hand rests on my shoulder and I look up as she leans over, her breasts bulging and her red lips arrowing in on my cheek. Her soft kiss leaves its mark, sticky and warm, and I pull her down to me.

* * * *

Look at this snooty cunt here – how does people's physical appearance reflect their attitudes so perfectly? The narrow, pointed beak on this fucker – it's built to sneer, built to look down on the world around it. Couldn't you just crack your knuckles across that nose, hanging out there, asking for it?

He's barely with it, this old geezer. Eyes drooping shut, pursed lips and sallow cheeks sinking into sagging jowls, which descend into a scrawny turkey neck. I watch as his head rocks to one side, collapsing over itself. There's a gentle snap as something gives way and his head lolls precariously. Still he sleeps.

I look more carefully; he's not in a good way, this guy. Skin yellowing by the moment and his features ballooning. No, this isn't right. His head begins to expand, gaining mass but losing weight. It strains upwards against the sagging neck, pulling away until it's air borne, tethered by the feeble tendons that once held it more firmly in place. Soon it's rising high above me, looking down, it's giant, yellow features indistinct, grotesque.

I watch as, from the mind now liberated, come pouring scenes of foulness, decay, and sex: men whose skin peels from their bodies, girls who gnaw on the slivers as they drop from the men. Finally, a goddess rises, her face buried in the looming crotch of an unseen man. Blood drips from unseen wounds, showering the world below. It's pornography, it's truth.

A swarm of locusts begin to cover the face as it deflates, scrabbling as they're drawn into the now hollow cheeks. The weight returns and the guy's head descends back to earth, smoothly settling on the ground at his feet, neck stretched but still attached.

* * * *

Do cinemas employ sarky little fuckers on purpose, or does the sugar sweet smell of the light fantastic foyers just draw them in? With Lex under my arm these things hardly register, but the little shit at the counter wasn't half taking his time about booking in our seats: 'There isn't a showing at quarter past; *quarter to* if you like', 'No, you can't have an aisle seat; they're all taken', 'Is that two adults?' – smarmy git. Spent the whole time staring at Lexi's bangers too – fair play to the lad, she's hardly covered up, but have a little decency, pal.

Still, what can you expect when you're with a stunner? Even the girl at the popcorn stand took an eyeful, couldn't help herself – never mind the guy checking tickets. It's par for the course when you've got a hot piece on your arm, and they don't come any hotter than Lexi.

The darkness of the cinema is a relief though; sat next to Lexi, my arm around her neck, our legs brushing up against one another. The ads that race across the screen

– confusing the senses, irritating the mind – reflect in Lexi's eyes, the lit images dancing across her face and highlighting the shape of her features, down to her gently heaving bosom.

I run my forefinger along her right leg – feel the pleasurable tingle run up the back of my neck to my head. She grasps my hand and, smiling, plants a peck on my cheek. It's good to have her back. It's the simple stuff you miss; the truly intimate.

I settle back and watch as the screen ignites in colour. A man with a fine teak-finish flashes a white hot smile. He reclines on a charcoal sofa in an empty flat. Smooth tones ease across the cinema, as his mobile phone rings. He answers it and the scene dissolves; the man transported to a different place, a bar filled with attractive people – his friends, a woman. He looks around, smiles. The tagline streaks across the screen: 'The new Sentio: Bringing you closer'. I let my head rock back in the chair, look over at Lex's cleavage from the new angle, and allow the music of the chirpy adverts to wash over me: false realties created to sell you lifestyle products for a lifestyle no one has.

* * * *

My hand prickles with nervous energy, dampness beginning to spread out from my palm. I flex my knuckles, watch as tendon and vein pop out, stressed.

"You ready?"

I look up, thick tar swilling around my brain as I do. This scrawny fucker – his skin clinging to the bones of his face, black eyes sunk back into his head as though retreating from the world, refusing to take in any more – he's no match for a true slinger like me.

"Said you ready, kid?"

The flex of his jaw gives away his anxiety, the constant grating a sign of his discomfort in stillness. I breathe him in, look deep into those eyes, drag them back to the reality that we're both faced with.

"Ready."

I smile, but breath comes unnaturally and my chest feels heavy. I refuse to let it show, refuse to be affected.

Turning to his right, the guy reaches out to a girl standing beside us. She's in tight denim jeans, cut off at the top of her juicy, well-reared thighs. I smile, and eye the gentle curve of her arse. An all-American arse; thick, unashamed. She hands each of us a Smith & Wesson Model 29. The smooth shaft shoots cooling shivers over my body as I cup it in my hand, calming my senses. With my other hand, I clasp the grip and slide a tentative finger through the guard and rest it softly on the trigger.

I look over to this joker in his trench coat. He's facing down his weapon too, getting to know it, feeling its contours, and making it his own. "Nice piece," he mutters.

I shrug, roll my shoulders. Lethal force is lethal force. "This loaded?" I ask.

"Sure," breathes the girl, exhaling the word through barely parted lips.

I smile. My opposite smiles. Squaring our shoulders,

we face one another.

"You know the rules, kid?"

What's with this guy – there's no kid here, no interloper. This is the real deal, the only truth.

"Ten paces," I say, smiling, "then," raising my finger, I blow an imagined hole straight through this loser's jacket and into his heart.

He nods. I smile. The nervous twitch in his jaw returns – the first sign that it had abated for a few moments.

Leaning in, the juicy dame plants a kiss on this guy's cheek – her soft lips leaving a smudged pink trace. It's a bad look to die in. "Good luck, Travis," she simpers.

I'm going to enjoy this, enjoy the final pace, the moment of uncertainty: glorious relief, light and unstoppable; or the weight of burden, of continued existence beyond the trigger – one awaits, one was never really an option in the first place. The moment between your ninth step and your tenth is euphoric, unmatchable.

His Mohawk blown in a moveless atmosphere, Travis ushers the dame away.

She strides back, her long brown limbs carrying her away from danger.

He nods and we turn back on back, the urge to take the kill shot only held back by the ten euphoric steps to come. Arms loose at my side, I feel the tension seep away – eyes averted, there's nothing left to fear. As my empty hand dangles free, it brushes briefly against Travis's – at least, it feels like his hand, but it could just as easily have been the butt of his Smith & Wesson, the fleeting touch not sufficient to tell if it was living flesh or cold metal that shot a spark of connection through me.

I crank my neck, start to focus. A sharp snap as the game's mistress clicks her fingers together. Both Travis and I stride forward, away from one another but closer towards our cosmic alignment. Another snap carries us still further on our shared journey.

The ache between each cracking of the silence becomes heavier as we move towards our final beat. Saliva builds in my mouth and I gulp it down on every half-beat. Blood rushes about my head; this is the final chance to run free, to opt out. One step to our destiny, one final snap travelling towards us through time and space to this moment, to the fingers of our oppressor. One final chance for redemption.

Snap. I spin, the gun rising swiftly through the thick air. I see Travis's back, his shoulders arching as he turns, and I clasp the trigger.

A clunk from the gun's chamber, but no explosion. I squeeze the trigger again, and the gun emits a high whining noise. Fucking Yank pistols. I look up, see Travis laughing, bent double with mirth. I squeeze again, but nothing more happens. I look down at my weapon, and watch as the tip of the shaft begins to wilt, gravity pulling it downwards in limp surrender. Tears roll from Travis's eyes as the gun becomes soft and useless in my hand. Piece of crap, useless piece of badly-made crap. I fling the weapon down and raise my hands. Travis stops laughing. The girl moves to his side and he pulls her close, his arms wrapping around her pillowy waist. Raising his weapon, he pulls the trigger. I stare down the long shaft as a bullet hurtles out towards me; the only end I could have hoped for.

Cold metal meets flesh and I breathe again.

* * * *

I lean back on the bar, my elbows pressing against the sticky wood.

"Nice," Matty calls, as a red drops into the far pocket.

"Jammy git," Jim responds.

Jimbo's never has been good at pool. Whether the balls are pixelated or real, he's just not got the eye for it. It's geometry, pool. Plain and simple. If you don't see the angles, it doesn't matter how well you execute. Pythagoras would have loved this shit.

Matty bends over the table to take his next shot. Cue gently rehearsing, he focuses his energy on the white ball, visualising the shot. With a smooth swiftness, he draws the cue back and, pausing a millisecond at the peak of his swing, brings it forward. The hard crack of ball hitting ball, and the red hurtles towards the corner, while the white spins off on its own trajectory, its motion no longer in line with the universe of the table; it's an errant star, refusing the pull of gravity. Matty watches the red ball from his bent position, chin on cue. It glides swiftly towards the gaping pocket. We all look on, but the satisfying plop never comes. Instead there's a cushioned thud of polished resin on skin, as the ball slaps Jim's palm, which now covers the pocket.

"Oi, wanker," Matty says. "That counts."

He goes to swipe the ball in with his cue but Jim intercepts with his own. Grinning, he pushes one of the yellow balls into the pocket instead.

"There you go," he offers.

A swift jab and Matty's cue prods Jim's softening gut, "Such a wanker."

Jim laughs and bends to take his shot. Matty turns and hands me the cue, "I need a drink," he says. "Finish this retard off for me."

I accept the order and four shots later the game is over. He's no Pythagoras, Jim.

With three fresh pints sitting on the table's scratched wooden edge, we insert another pound coin and listen to the internal commotion as the balls race towards either end of the table, the game reset.

"Ready to get spanked again, bitch?" Matty says.

Jim rolls his eyes as Matty starts ordering the freshly released balls into the plastic triangle. With a swift and silent flick, Jim smacks his cue across the back of Matty's legs. A few balls make a break for freedom, one plunging back into the darkness of the table's hidden tunnels, as Matty is jolted with the momentary shock.

He turns, sending one of the pints toppling to the floor. A muted cheer as the glass smashes, and Matty grabs Jim in a headlock. It's only a laugh, but Jim struggles furiously, laughing but powerless.

"Watch it," the barman calls, as he leaves his station and approaches the spillage.

I leap onto Matty's back and we all crumple into a mess on the floor. The barman shoos us out of the way, but we only laugh.

He sweeps the broken glass and spilled booze to one side, and we offer our least sincere apologies. Cues back in hand, the game commences once more.

* * * *

Her soft, pink tongue caresses her top lip, wiping away tiny beads of sweat and replacing them with warm saliva. Looking up with heavily mascaraed eyes, her lips slightly parted, she breathes deeply. Her soft fingers brush the tender skin of my belly as she searches out the buckle to my belt. Finding it, she pulls it open and slowly begins to slide my jeans and boxers down in one movement. As the scratchy curls of my pubes bristle against the material, her eyes drop, slowly, to my waist; millimetre by millimetre, the thick base of my cock begins to show, and she licks her lips in anticipation. As more and more of my heavy shaft is revealed, I can sense her breaths growing shorter, more agitated. Her wrists rub my thighs as she hauls my jeans down, and I can feel the tiny hairs on my legs stand to attention, following the erection straining to be released.

With more than seven inches of powerful cock revealed, she looks up once more, eyes wide now, delight and fear mingling behind the dilated pupils. Refusing to continue the tease, she drags my jeans the remaining distance and liberates the giant erection. She gapes as the heavy penis – thicker than her wrist – dangles in front of her, inviting, dangerous. Wrapping her moist lips around the swinging tip, she strokes her tongue over the bulbous end, desperate to come to terms with this freak of nature.

I allow her only a few moments' pleasure before I hoist her up by the armpits and fling her back on to the bed. Spreading her legs wide, I thrust the enflamed erection deep into her cunt. She screams as the many inches of swollen flesh stretch and tear at her tender folds. The noise only encourages the flow of blood, and soon I'm swelling inside her, the already unbearable girth expanding, pressing against every part of her aching pussy. She tries to sit up, to protest the action, but I force her down as I attempt to manoeuvre in and out of her quickly reddening twat.

Looking down to try and find her clit – to send her over the edge – I take in the swollen and stretched skin around her pussy, note the tiny fractural nicks that emerge from the once smooth skin. Looking up at her reddening face, a pulsing vein showing in her forehead, I feel the weight of my cock increase again, growing up infinitely now, tearing at her insides, taking her to places she's never been before. The cutting rawness of her screams forces me ever deeper, the walls of her vagina bursting to allow me access to more and more of her, the throbbing tip of my cock exploring the soft innards, so often hidden.

Trying to ease the giant implement between my legs even a fraction out, I realise that we're stuck in this dance, powerless to relinquish the grapple while blood flows. Looking down at the base of my cock, I note that it's got to be at least eight inches across now, this dame's legs spreading ever wider, trying to incorporate the swelling member. Anxiety begins to hit; I try to pull away, to escape. But there is no escape. The soft belly of this girl is stretching now, ballooning up as the volume inside her inflates further and further. Bloated with my offering, the skin on her stomach expands, covered with violent stretch marks. Her navel pops and, from within, I can feel the warm gush of blood as her organs are rearranged to accommodate the unstoppable manhood within. Her eyes roll, and I expect her to faint, but she hangs in there. A terrible tearing sound cuts across her screams, and I look down as her pussy lips part and a rip runs up, through her clit and to her lower abdomen. All the time, I continue to expand, continue to grow to new heights.

One final scream and her whole belly explodes open, blood splattering outwards as my savage cock – swollen to the size of a small tree trunk – bursts free. Her head collapses backwards, lifeless, and I stroke the taut bulk of my weapon. Everything is red.

* * * *

Blackness looms, racing towards me. Or perhaps I'm racing towards it. Gusts rush in my ears, and my head spins.

Two soft, purple lines hang in the air – the centre of the blackness, my only point of reference. They grow bigger and bigger as they draw near; the rushing in my ears getting higher and higher, louder and louder.

The purple lines – vertical and enormous – slow, begin to drift towards me, fearful in their assured progression. I reach out to press them away, to fight off the blackness, but my hands fall into it, through the blackness and into more darkness. Reaching up, I try to grasp onto the purple strips once more – a perfect 'pause' sign above my head – but find that they're not there. It's a trick of the senses, the purple strips are feet away in the blackness – no, miles away. Flailing, my hands sink through the noxious blackness and find nothing solid.

Tumbling to my knees, I feel the dank, desperate blackness roll over me, consume me. My knees find no place to rest, but simply sink downwards, or perhaps backwards, through the dark.

I look up, and the strips of purple remain. I claw at the dark, clutch it to my face and bury myself in it, trying to force out the light and allow the blackness free reign. The light dims and I breathe heavy, thankful breaths.

* * * *

Pure, voluminous whiteness surrounds me. Soft, inviting, I sink into its folds, feel it embrace my naked skin. It wraps itself around me, comforting me, hiding me. I curl into a tight ball and feel the cotton soft whiteness follow my movement.

Clasping it tightly in my fists, I feel it pulling away from me, trying to escape. A sharp yank and it's gone. I look up and see Lexi, her warm brown body as naked as mine. She smiles and climbs into the luxurious double bed beside me. I pull her close, the sweet softness of her skin soothing my own. She pulls the duvet back over us and whiteness hides us from the world once more.

"You smell fantastic," I whisper.

She turns towards me and breathes warm, sweet air onto my face. I hold her close and breathe in the scent of her hair, feel the curves of her body pressed against me.

"Let's stay here forever," I say.

She mumbles agreement.

* * * *

The sharp sea air stings my face, a breath catching in my chest as I fight the urge to gasp at the cold. The rolling and crashing of waves below my feet is disorienting, my head swims and my senses dull. Glancing down through the rough wooden boards of the pier I see the mass of heaving blue and feel the instability of my position. Legs weak, I look up, trying to gather my senses. The orange sunlight that fractures the darkening sky sends flashes of colour across my vision. Quickly sickening, I stagger forward, ready to tumble over.

I steady myself, grasping my knees with my hands. The nausea subsides slightly. Bringing my head up, I watch as the people around me glide past, seemingly weightless. Indifference on their faces, they look straight on, uninterested. Faces shimmering a sickly green in the dying light, they have eyes only for one another – for their fellows.

I spin about, wonder if one of them will stop. The landscape spins and I lose balance. I fall.

* * * *

A succulent, pink pork chop lays gently dribbling juices onto the crisp white plate. A cluster of runner beans, and three new potatoes sit apart, each a distinct part of the meal.

"Eat up, son."

I look up. To my right, and stuffed into a light pink pullover, is Marlon Brando. In a getup like that you'd think he'd be embarrassed, squirming like a motherfucker, but no – he's calm, looking down at me with easy affection.

I cut a small triangle from the pork, slip it into my dry mouth and chew. Brando winks at me. Fucking weird: who winks in real life?

"Is it good?"

I turn to my left. Susan Sarandon – her hair in loose ringlets – looks eagerly over to me.

"Yeah, it's fine," I venture.

She smiles, and folds her arms across her comfortable bust. She wears a light pink cardigan – the double of Brando's jumper.

I take another bite, and she reaches down to squeeze my forearm reassuringly, "Good boy."

"Hey, kid, what d'you say we shoot down the store after dinner and pick up some things for the weekend? I need a couple of strong arms to help carry the stuff about," Brando says.

Fuck this; these two are clearly off their fucking rockers. It ain't the 1950s and I'm definitely not a Stepford son. They can just wind their necks in and act straight.

"Oh yes, help Dad, would you, son? I'll straighten things up here, and then maybe I could come too – would that be ok by you, Mick?" Sarandon says, her face all but expressionless.

"That'd be fine, dandelion."

Fucking sickening.

* * * *

"Caviar, sir?"

The waiter is incredulous, eyeing me like he's going to make me back down.

"Beluga Caviar," I confirm.

"It's nine thousand pounds a serving, sir."

There's a question in his voice, but I only smile: "Yes."

This greasy fuck loiters, hanging about as though waiting for some moment of clarity to set in and things to be made clear, for me to crawl back down some hole where I must have come from.

I reach into my suit pocket and pull out a small wad of fifty pound notes. I toss them up to him, and turn back to the table. He scurries off, and I wonder what Beluga Caviar is like.

* * * *

Now just look at this dame here – that's what you call a stunner. Have you ever seen a body as fucking stacked as that? Pale skin running smooth as silk over a gentle frame but erupting into spectacular curves at places. This is what women should look like. This is real femininity, real sex.

Soft curls hanging about her face, dark lips and penetrating eyes breaking up the pallor of her skin. She's dangerous, a true pinup, a true corrupter. Look at this now, her breasts squeezed together between those feeble arms, bursting out as firm, full orbs. You don't get knockers like that too often. Look at the nipples too: succulent, pointing forward in agonised arousal. Couldn't you just clamp your jaws around them? Fuck.

Her arms back at her sides, those epic breasts sag. Each sinking a few inches lower than desirable, visibly deflating. The peachy nipples fall southwards, pointing down towards the belly, once smooth but now creasing, the firm skin crumpling into a matted tangle of fat. New weight straining on the belly and pulling it down, a flap of blubber collapses over itself and conceals the whole pubic region, making a eunuch of this object of sex.

Beneath the once inviting cunt, the pinup's pins bulge, her thighs riddled with cellulite and swelling outwards in crumpled mounds. As I look up at her face, now hollow, I see the grey hue that's falling over the once sun-ripe skin, the sweet brown replaced with a cardboard grey. Clumps of hair fall from her head and land at her feet, which are now curling inwards, the toes crooked and all acting on separate instructions.

Above her breasts, the harsh points of bones deform her chest, the soft curves replaced with violent distortions to the landscape. Her eyes sink back into her head and her lips purse to the point, almost, of non-existence. Only a few tufts of withered hair remain on her scalp, and her face resembles a skull more than a person.

Her spine crooks and she leans forwards, her heavy breasts swinging down and free. The frail ankles that keep her upright, buckle. She collapses forwards, grasping out at me as she falls. I look on, unmoved.

* * * *

It's a narrow reality, out here, with these 'people'. They just don't see where we're headed, where the next step of evolution takes us. Living mechanical lives, they already exist apart, alone, they don't want anything else – and yet they continue with the pretence. It's us progressives who get left out in the cold. It's always been the way – the world discards and disregards those that it can't cope with, those who move outside the standard pattern.

It's down to us select few to take the next step, to realise our own authenticity and shake this place up a bit. They haven't got a clue, but we're poised to take over, to live the new life, the real life, the atomic life. One day, they'll look back and wonder how they ever thought they could continue in their delusion, how only the few grasped true freedom. The revolution is coming: it's inevitable, unstoppable, it breathes.

* * * *

The coarse cotton of the tablecloth soothes my warm palm as I caress the folds that hang by my knees. The hum of activity all around is indistinct, a wall of noise – I have eyes, and ears, only for Lex. Her damp lips glisten as we lock gazes. Reaching across the table, she places her hand on mine and looks me straight in the eye as she smiles; a warm, generous smile. I return it, and we settle in our bubble.

A moment of stillness, and then Lexi's lips part, and she speaks:

"I love you."

The warmth of her words spreads across my body, relaxing my muscles and causing an ache to grow up in my chest.

"I love you too," I say.

She smiles.

* * * *

The darkness surrounds me, pressing in and suffocating my senses; a dying place, cold and indifferent. This world is blind to me, and I to it. We've said our goodbyes, dropped all pretences. The illusion is dead, long live the illusion.

My hand reaches out, and I grasp blindly.

Light floods the room, and this world fades behind me.

The comforting whirr: a space ship that takes me outside of time or space.

I embrace reality.

Matthew Selwyn is a young writer from London, England. His debut novel, ****: *The Anatomy of Melancholy* was released in 2014. A student and librarian, he is often to be found hiding amongst the stacks in the Victorian library where he works, surrounded by piles of books.

He writes book reviews online at www.bibliofreak.net.

www.matthewselwyn.com